HAMMERHEAD

This is a work of fiction. All of the characters and events portrayed in this novel are either products of the authors' imagination or are used fictitiously.

Hammerhead
ISBN: 978-1-947018-36-5

For More Information Contact:

Three Kings Publishing
115 Canterbury Court
Princeton, Kentucky 42445
threekingspublishing@gmail.com

HAMMERHEAD

by Ryan King

Three Kings Publishing

To Jesus Christ, my Savior and my King

Jesus declared, “Love the Lord your God with all your heart and with all your soul and with all your mind.” Matthew 22:37

Chapter 1

Cairn, Kentucky
August 1977

Poor lambs, Denise thought. That is what they were. She looked out over the small classroom, saw the boys and girls under her special care. Denise Simms was raised on a sheep farm far to the northeast of this little Kentucky town. She understood poor lost creatures. The ones that were weak or deformed or sickly. The innocent and vulnerable who were rejected through no fault of their own and had to be bottle fed in order to even have a chance at survival. Those lambs, if they survived, were grateful for the love and security but always seemed to have a sense of confused sadness about them. Wondering why they were not like others or loved the same.

Just like these children.

Retarded is what the ignorant called them, mostly without malice, but not always. Mentally disabled was the more acceptable term among the educated but the terms were still only shorthand for a heartbreak so deep and unfair that it made you want to cry out to the heavens. A heartbreak she was witness to every day. Like the broken lambs she had raised, there was only so much she could do. Especially as an outsider in a place like Cairn, Kentucky.

The worst part is she could almost glimpse the person they could have been. *Even with all our faults we are still beautiful at times*, she thought. *These children are no different.*

"Five minutes," Denise told the class. Most were done already, or as done as they would ever be. Her fellow teachers saw her as little more than a baby-sitter and viewed her efforts at teaching these children, and her assessments to gauge any progress, as absurd at best. She didn't want to think of what they might think of her efforts at their worst. They possibly thought her cruel, expecting too much from the broken. Denise tried not to dwell on what others thought of her, but that had always been a losing game for her.

She had arrived here by chance. The government had picked Cairn in the Appalachian foothills of eastern Kentucky for her to teach as the flip side of the bargain for paying her college costs. It was an initiative by the new southern democratic president Jimmy Carter to help rural schools close the education gap with their more advanced urban counterparts. Denise would not have come to such a place on her own, and the locals certainly would not have chosen her. Although it was never said, she understood her position perfectly. Outsider.

A faint and welcome breeze flittered through the open windows. She took a moment to acknowledge that it was a beautiful day. The beginning of a new school year and the last days of summer. The sun's rays were so tangibly golden and warm that one could imagine running their fingers through them. Dust motes floated lazily in the air with all the glory of galaxies. Robins, bluejays and finches chirped joyfully in the nearby trees with more harmony than an orchestra.

Movement caught her eye and she looked back to the class at an unusually large boy, truly a lost sheep if there ever was one. He was writing on his assessment test with a level of concentration and attention she found surprising. Both were often in short supply in her class. The boy looked up and caught her gazing at him. Denise smiled reassuringly but Caleb Woods frowned and unconsciously turned so the deformed part of his head was more hidden from her view.

Hammerhead. That was what the kids called him. She didn't know why and didn't care. Like most kids here he wore second-hand clothes patched and altered by seasoned women who knew survival depended on not wasting any resource. Caleb wasn't just tall for his age but also muscular and bulky with dark hair and eyes. If things had been slightly different Caleb would have been the star of the football team with all the popularity such things came with. But Caleb Woods was obviously different, that was painfully easy for the world to see.

He kept his hair as long as school rules allowed in order to hide his deformity. The left side of his skull was not round but dented in as if someone had taken a scoop of skull and brain from him. No hair grew along the birth defect, just a dark purple weal that appeared to embody pain.

Principal Johnson had warned her about Caleb at her initial counseling session. Told her the boy was born this way and was missing part of his brain, "Miracle he's even alive." He told her that Caleb Woods was obviously mentally disabled and would never be successful at learning more than basic letters, numbers, and simple concepts. The principal chuckled when she asked about his reading ability. He told her to just keep an eye on him. While most of the children in her Special Education class were harmless, Caleb Woods had been known to become angry and disruptive at times, sometimes to the point of requiring paddling, which always put the boy back in his place. "Still," Principal Johnson added, "I advise caution around that boy and recommend you not to be alone with him. Just in case." He then smiled and waved her out of his office. "No need to be concerned, you'll be fine."

"One minute," she announced. "Please finish up and make sure your name and date are at the top." Denise scanned the room and knew that probably only about half of the class would manage that skill but was committed to teaching them as much as they could absorb. Committed to loving them and wanting the best for them.

"Time is up," she said just before the bell rang and habitual, institutionalized bedlam of released students ensued. "Turn in your papers," she yelled out over the kids standing, talking, and making their way into the hall. It was the last period so most of them were motivated to exit the room with more urgency than if there had been a fire.

Standing at the room's only exit she collected the papers, smiling at each child. Most smiled back with honesty and appreciation. *This is the most important thing I can teach them*, she thought, *that they are seen, loved, and matter. Anything else is just bonus credit.*

She tried to keep this thought in mind as the papers grew in her hand. Most had a great deal of blank space. A few only had their name. Many were blank. She would work on that. They had time. Their minds, however disadvantaged, were not recalcitrant, unlike many of their "normal" classmates, which was why Denise had requested this assignment once she arrived in Cairn. At least the special children wanted to learn. For the most part.

Denise felt a shadow hover over her and looked up. Caleb Woods always seemed bigger when he was standing. In the classroom chair he managed to shrink down, perhaps to hide his deformed head, but it tended to have the opposite effect.

His dark eyes downcast, he attempted to slip by her and out the door. She stepped in front of him and held out her hand with a smile. He looked down at her, and Denise resisted the urge to step back. Caleb's eyes were not what she had come to expect among her students. These were eyes capable of calculation, perhaps even violence. She realized they were the last two in the classroom and the hallway behind her was nearly empty now. She was alone with him.

"Your paper, Caleb," she said forcing her voice to be relaxed and calm. She had learned that children tended to mimic the emotional tenor of adults for better or worse. "Please," she added with a smile.

He stared at her for a long moment, his large brow knotted. Finally, he reached into his pocket and pulled out a folded piece of paper. Before he placed it into her hand he crushed it into a small ball and dropped it into her hand. He then brushed rudely past her into the hallway and strode towards the exit.

Letting out her pent-up breath, Denise placed the papers on her desk and began smoothing out the paper Caleb had given her. She was not surprised to find it was totally blank and dropped the paper into her trashcan. Sitting down at her desk she placed the papers neatly in front of her but her eyes were drawn outside. Denise Woods wondered if she were wasting her time.

"Teach?" Principal Johnson had asked incredulously. "You won't be able to teach these kids anything other than how to go to the bathroom and to be quiet in church." He shook his head at her with a frown. "No, Miss Woods, those retards you have will likely be removed from school by their parents as soon as they are large enough to hire out as farm labor or for logging. That's not a bad living for them. They'll never need to know how to read or do math, just keep them out of everyone else's way."

In the days after this interaction with her new boss, she had thought of many things to say in return. Speeches on human dignity and the sanctity of every life and the profound task of every teacher to educate. But she said nothing. She told herself it was because she had been shocked by the man's backwardness. His casual meanness. The truth was that she rarely thought of relevant or even witty responses at the time. Those only came later when they were useless. As a guilty repudiation.

Denise shook her head and forced herself to take a deep breath. She stacked the papers in front of her, looked out over the empty classroom and froze.

Caleb. He had spent the entire class writing. She remembered the concentration. She stood and reached into her trash to pick up the paper. It was blank. She flipped it over to the back and her breath caught.

It was a drawing. Not some doodle-like thing she had seen a million times. It clearly showed a young woman staring into the sun with an easy smile on her face. The sun's beams kissed her skin lightly. The curves and shading were perfect. There were no corrections or imperfections. It was not a drawing, it was art. It was beautiful. The woman was beautiful.

Her knees felt weak and she settled down into her chair. "Oh, my," she said softly.

She realized the beautiful woman in the drawing was her.

Chapter 2

Caleb strode towards his escape looking neither right nor left. There was no point in making eye contact, most would avoid it and he had long ago learned to only expect ridicule, pity, or fear.

The Buttheads were the exception. Vic Brown, Gus Evans, and Norm Nettles, known as Moose for his size and disposition, didn't avoid eye contact with him, they sought him out among others. The Buttheads is what he had taken to calling the older bullies.

Darting his eyes quickly to either side, Caleb stepped through the hallway doors and out into the playground. He heard the Buttheads before he saw them. Their cruel laughter indicated they had secured prey for their afterschool torment. Vic, Gus, and Moose formed a halfmoon around a confused smiling boy with his back to the brick wall.

Caleb identified the boy as Timmy Dorn from his classes. Timmy was slow in the head but always cheerful and happy. Downs syndrome was the term adults whispered. Timmy was the sort of person that drove the Buttheads into a rage and ignited their thirst for meanness.

Caleb stopped and looked at them. He was torn between a desire to help and the need to flee.

If they had glanced over at that moment the decision might have been made for him, but they were focused on the small happy boy. Caleb's fists clenched but guilt filled him. He knew he would leave no matter how much he wanted to fight.

"Hey, what's going on here?"

Caleb turned to the door he had just exited and saw Miss Denise Simms standing there. She moved towards the boys without a hint of hesitation or fear. She stepped into the circle and put her arm around Timmy. When she looked up with an angry look, the Buttheads had already drifted away.

Even this small woman has more courage than I do, Caleb thought.

Inwardly fuming, Caleb turned away and resumed his purposeful walk across the school grounds. He felt rather than saw the eyes that touched him as he made his way through the town's small center. The restaurant, coffee shop, and clothing store patrons frowned when they saw him before looking away. Caleb pulled his head down closer to his neck to try and hide his deformity behind his backpack while putting his wool sock cap on his head. He always felt as if he were either in the spotlight or invisible. There was no chance of anything in between. No chance of normal.

The town center gave way to upscale residential streets that in turn gave way to railroad tracks, warehouses, and weed-filled parking lots. Caleb ducked off the street onto a small dirt path. He stooped to step under the low-hanging limbs and climbed steadily upwards. The temperature instantly dropped and the entire world became quieter, calmer. Caleb stopped and closed his eyes while pulling the hot sock cap off his head. After a few seconds of stillness, he heard the birds and squirrels resume their busy lives. He opened his eyes and continued on with light steps, not wanting to disturb anything.

Climbing up the path he came to an open grassy area half the size of a football field. The edges were ringed by trees, stubborn bushes, and brambles. A line of ageless hills highlighted by the bright summer light ringed the horizon. If he had walked out into the field and turned west Caleb could have seen the high somber stone buildings of Cairn State Penitentiary. He was not so inclined. Instead, he sat in his normal spot, his back to an old walnut tree. It was the best view.

Opening his backpack, he pulled out a small paper sack and laid out pieces of bread from his lunch on his thighs. Caleb put the sack away and then sat very still, breathing only when he needed to.

He had almost dozed off when he heard the small rustling behind his head and resisted the urge to turn. Quick clicking movements interrupted by silence. Something brushed against his shoulder and then there was a small warm weight on his arm. And then almost as if by magic the squirrel was on his lap eating the bread. The faintest hint of a smile crossed Caleb's face and all the tension and doubt and heartache in the world melted away.

The squirrel grabbed the bread crust and jumped down to the ground but didn't go far. It sat on its back legs holding the bread in its front paws and eating. Shiny dark eyes watched Caleb. Its bushy tail was up and occasionally twitched. Caleb recognized this squirrel from the small white patch like a star under its chin. He called this one Rocky.

He heard faint stirrings further up in the tree wondering if Rocky's companion, Smoke, would join them. Caleb was not surprised when the other squirrel remained up high. Smoke was not as courageous, or foolish, as Rocky. The squirrel finished its snack, sniffed around the ground for a few seconds looking for anything it had missed, and then its tail shook excitedly and it raced across the ground and back up the tree.

Why can't it be like this all the time, he wondered. *Just me and the animals. They don't care what I look like. Only the people care that I'm a mistake.*

A mistake. To be born this way. He pondered the familiar quandary. Either God made a mistake with Caleb, or God wanted him this way. Perhaps God didn't care one way or the other.

A pair of rabbits caught his attention across the meadow. They stayed under the edge of the trees for protection against hawks. The little rabbits were intent on eating dandelions. Caleb watched as they bit off the flowers at their base and then devoured the stem up towards the flower itself. They did this with such an air of peace and joy and contentment.

If only he could be one of these animals.

Moving ever so slowly, Caleb eased his notebook and a pencil out of his bag. Carefully flipping to an open page, he began to sketch the rabbits.

Chapter 3

Lord, I feel old today, Thomas McDaniel thought. He pulled the work gloves off his lined hands and wiped the damp grey hair from his brow. Looking up at the sky he saw it was a beautiful warm day.

"I'm sorry, Lord, I shouldn't complain, but I *am* old," he pointed at the massive limb that had fallen that afternoon blocking his driveway, "and this is not a task for an old man."

Thomas sat on the limb and sighed. "Is your hand in this? Maybe trying to tell me I need to exercise more? Or that instead of taking the car I should walk? Doctor Collins would tend to agree with you, said it would be good for my heart. Or maybe it's just a tree limb that falls as they do and you're chuckling at the presumption of a silly old man. A lonely old man at that," Thomas admitted.

"Who obviously feels a little too sorry for himself at times."

He stood and put the gloves back on his hands eyeing the limb. "Lord, if you're not going to miracle this limb out of the way for me, please give me the strength and wisdom to figure this thing out." Walking around the large maple limb he again assessed the task. "This would be easier work if I had a chainsaw. And if I knew how to operate a chainsaw. Probably just as well, I'd likely end up cutting off my leg. Perhaps I could burn it in place," he looked at the overhanging limbs from the nearby trees. "No, that would be foolish, especially as dry as everything is." Thomas grabbed the end of the limb with a good hold, squatted with his legs, and pulled. The limb hardly budged at all. He did feel a warning twinge in his lower back and knew from experience if he kept this up he'd be bedridden for a few days and miserable.

An urge to go inside and have a drink suddenly came upon him but he resisted it. The urge to drink was nearly always worse when he was either lonely or dejected. But he knew from experience what one drink would do. One drink would become another and then too many. The rest of the day and night would be lost in melancholy and sad memories, and the next morning would begin with fatigue, regret, and shame.

Thomas laughed suddenly and shook his grey head. "No, God, I'm not going to make a bad situation worse, I hope those days are behind me. I'm sure you feel the same, not to presume the mind of the Almighty, of course, but I suspect you could do without my occasional stubborn prideful willfulness."

A verse came to him as they tended to do in times like this. *My grace is sufficient for you, for my power is made perfect in weakness.* Thomas nodded and bowed his head. The realization and peace filled him, and the tension slowly went out of his shoulders. Letting out a breath he looked up and saw a large boy walking down the street in front of his house. He would have mistaken him for a man except for the bookbag on his back. Curiously, he was wearing a wool sock hat in eighty-degree weather.

"Hey, son," Thomas called out without thinking. The boy kept walking. "Hey there, big fella. Can you give me a hand?"

The boy stopped and turned. His dark eyes held suspicion and his feet shuffled as if they wanted to keep walking. Thomas noticed that the hat rested strangely on the boy's head as if he had something stuffed up under the right side of his head.

He waved the boy over. "Come on, I won't bite you. I know your generation hasn't been raised to help their elders but let me show you the way." Thomas laughed at his own joke and the laughter appeared to break the boy's paralysis. Looking up and down the street first, he stepped onto Thomas's driveway and walked up to the base of the massive limb, eyeing it intently. Thomas realized that the boy was as tall as he was and the old man was taller than most. The boy also easily out-weighted him by a hundred pounds and none of it looked like fat.

"Alrighty," Thomas said pointing. "We need to work together. We'll get on each side of the limb's base. I'll count to three and we can lift together." He pointed to the shed behind his small two-story house. "We'll drag it back there were I keep the other limbs, although this one is a little larger than I'm used to. It's heavy so we can stop and take breaks if we need to." Looking down at his hands and then at the boy's he had a realization and snapped his fingers. "Hold on just a second, buddy, I've got another pair of gloves in the shed."

Turning away he began walking quickly towards the back of his house. He didn't want the boy to escape until the job was finished. The attention span of kids these days wasn't what it had once been. A heavy rustling sound caused him to turn, and he expected to see the boy fleeing down the driveway.

Instead, the boy was walking backwards towards him with his large legs and back knotted. He had the base of the large limb in his hands and had managed to lift it off the ground on his own. More incredible still he was dragging it backwards by himself. Not as a struggle, but as a simple, moderately challenging task. Thomas stepped out of the way before he could be dragged along like debris.

"That works too," Thomas said smiling. The boy's eyes darted up at him but seemed to relax when he saw no meanness. Thomas followed the boy as he dragged the large limb beside the shed and dropped it towards the back. Without having to be told, he walked around to the limb's side, squatted down to get a good hold on the outlying limbs, and lifted upwards pushing the branches towards the shed.

The old man nodded. "You do good work, son, and I appreciate the help." He pulled off his gloves and stuck out his hand, "Thomas McDaniel."

The boy hesitated, feet shuffled, but the societal importance of politeness was not something that could be ignored. He slowly reached out his massive hand and took Thomas's. He gave it a little shake and attempted to let go but the old man held on.

"What's your name son? Men can't trust each other unless they know each other's names. Now, your great and kind deed today speaks of your generosity and Samson-like strength, but names are important."

The boy looked at Thomas with a mixture of suspicion and fear. The boy's grip tightened for a second and Thomas wondered if the boy was dangerous. Then it relaxed. "Caleb. Caleb Woods…sir."

"Nice to meet you, Caleb." Thomas let go of the boy's hand. "That's a fine name. Caleb was a hero of the Old Testament and one of the few Hebrews who trusted God when everyone else doubted. Did you know that?"

The boy shook his head and looked towards the street longingly.

“Come up to the porch,” Thomas said putting an arm around Caleb’s shoulders. “Share a soda with me, it’s least I can do for the help you have given me.” The old man stopped in his tracks and smacked his head with a palm. “Forgetful old man,” he looked into Caleb’s eyes. “Have I said, ‘thank you’ yet?”

Caleb opened his mouth, but nothing came out.

“Never mind, doesn’t hurt to say it again. Thank you, young man,” he began steering Caleb towards the front of the house again. “You have done a good deed today and stored up treasure for yourself in heaven.” Thomas smiled and nodded his head as if answering his own question. He led Caleb up the porch stairs and pointed at a chair in the corner. “Better take that one, all the others are a little rickety and I don’t want you to end up on your butt.”

When Thomas emerged again with a coke bottle in each hand he found the large boy still standing. “Have a seat,” he said handing the boy the drink and then sitting himself. Caleb hesitated and then sat slowly and after a few moments he took a sip of his drink. “Nothing nicer on a warm summer day than sitting in the shade with a drink,” Thomas said while taking a long swallow.

There was a yell from down the street and then laughter and then more yelling. Thomas glanced over and saw Caleb stiffen. Soon three boys came into view walking in front of Thomas's house. They walked with the puffed-up false bravado of bullies everywhere. One of the boys looked up at the house and saw Caleb sitting on the porch.

"Look at that," he said pointing. "Hammerhead having a little drinkie with some old man."

The other boys turned and smiled evilly in their direction. "Hey there, Hammerhead, did your daddy hit you in the head with a hammer before he ran off and left you or was that after." Another yelled out, "Got your little baby hat on to cover your caved in head."

Thomas watched the boys and saw Caleb drop his head out of the corner of his eye.

"Don't look away," Thomas said sternly. "Never look away. See them for what they are and let them know you see them."

Caleb slowly looked up and stared at the boys. They threw a few more juvenile taunts but seemed unnerved by Caleb and the old man silently staring at them and quickly moved on down the street.

"Hammerhead," Thomas said. "They call you that because of your head?"

Caleb nodded.

Thomas sighed. "Clever I suppose. Mankind is always the cleverest in his cruelty." He looked over at Caleb. "If you don't mind me asking, what happened? To your head, I mean."

The boy sat silently for a long while staring at his coke. Finally, he spoke, "Born this way. Birth defect they say. Messed my head up."

"There's no shame, son," Thomas said. "Look at me."

Slowly the boy raised his head to meet Thomas's eyes.

He pointed at Caleb's head. "That's not your fault. This is a cruel and fallen world. Know that if it wasn't that, there would be something else they would try and use to tear you down. God made you perfectly and gloriously and we are all far more than what we look like, praise God!"

Caleb stared at him silently, but his coke shook a little in his hand.

"Will you take off that hat?" Thomas asked. "I'm not asking out of some ghoulish curiosity. I'm asking for you. That wool hat has to be like an oven on your head in this heat. I won't laugh or judge like those miscreants," Thomas said waving vaguely in the direction the boys had disappeared. "Can you trust me with seeing you?"

The boy sat silently looking at his feet.

Thomas set his soda down on the nearby table and stood up. He pulled his shirt out of his pants and up under his arm pits. He turned halfway to expose a series of ugly whelps, burns, and scar tissue on the old man's back. "See that?" he asked.

Caleb looked up and was staring at the scars with curiosity.

"Japanese prison guards did that to me, during the war."

"Why?" Caleb asked.

Thomas shrugged pulling the shirt back down and sitting. "That's a very complicated question. I suppose it was because I was an American and they could. Probably also because I was a chaplain…a priest, and I tried to help my fellow prisoners to not lose heart. Could just simply be because the Japanese were some of the most ruthless and sadistic sons-of-bitches the world has ever seen. At least until we kicked their asses. Please forgive my profanity, I'll need to confess and do penance for that."

The old man stared off into the distance for a moment before turning to the boy. "The point is, Caleb, those ugly scars are something that happened to me, they are not who I am, and they are not something I feel shame over. I have plenty of things to be ashamed of, believe me, but not over what happened to me. Neither should you over your scars."

Caleb slowly reached up and pulled the cap off his head and sat with his eyes down.

The old man studied him for a second and nodded. "I've seen much worse. You want another soda?" Without waiting for an answer, he went inside and came back with two more bottles. Caleb chugged the last of his first bottle before accepting the fresh drink. The old man was also holding out three dollars.

"Go on, take it." Thomas said seeing how the boy drew back suspiciously. "You earned it. Better yet you earned it without any guarantee of payment. I appreciate a generous heart, but I don't yet require charity."

Caleb slowly took the money and the old man sat back down. There was a pleasant comfortable silence between them as they enjoyed the day and their drinks.

"How would you like to earn some more money?" Thomas asked.

The boy looked at him with a questioning face.

The old man lifted one hand and waved around in the general direction of his porch, house, and yard. "I've got plenty that needs being done around here. The gutters should have been cleaned out months ago, but I'm nervous about getting on that ladder anymore. The windows need to be re-caulked and the shed painted. Lots of other things I've been putting off. I'll pay you a fair wage."

Caleb looked around at the yard as Thomas said these things. He then looked back at the money.

"It would be after school or on Saturdays, of course," the old man said. "Make sure and talk to your folks about it, not good to keep things like that from them. If they want to talk to me about it first, I'm okay with that."

"I better get home," Caleb said standing.

"Yes," Thomas answered standing and stuck his hand out again. "It has been a pleasure to meet you Mister Caleb Woods. Believe me when I say you have been the best thing that has happened to me today."

Caleb shook his hand, and then slowly walked down the front steps.

"See you tomorrow, my friend," Thomas said after him. He watched the boy march purposefully away and out of sight down the street.

"Well, that was something," Thomas said with a chuckle and noticed the boy's wool cap lying on the table beside the empty soda bottle.

Chapter 4

Helen Woods' hand shook as she brought the Pall Mall cigarette up to her lips. She took a long drag and then blew the smoke out slowly. Things were slipping, it couldn't be denied any longer. Helen knew what that meant. She did a good job of covering for herself, at least she hoped so, but more and more things were confusing. Time was fuzzy. Memories were reality and reality were memories. Her sister Alice had ultimately died from dementia a few years ago. Helen had watched the light in her sister's eyes be replaced by fear and confusion. It hadn't been long before she had simply withdrawn into herself and refused to eat or recognize those around her. Helen had a front row seat to that horrible and confusing decline.

"I won't go out like that," she croaked and then coughed roughly. She took a sip from the mason jar filled halfway with Old Grandad Whiskey. Her eyes wandered over to the top kitchen cabinet. Her dead husband Reuben's special pills were up there in a little box. The dangerous pain meds for when things had gotten really bad with his cancer. It would be easy to take a handful of those and just drift off to sleep forever.

"Not yet," she said looking away. "There's still time. Not that bad yet."

Her eyes roamed around the kitchen. The dishes from breakfast were still in the sink, and she hadn't swept the floor in days. She turned to look into the adjacent dining room and saw dust on the formal table. All things she had meant to do today, likely meant to do the day before, but she didn't want to think about that. Most of the day had slipped away, and she had no idea where she had been or what she had done. It was like her life was happening to someone else much of the time.

It's just been a bad day, Helen thought. *They're not all like this. Just ride the ups and downs. Maybe it will get better.* But Helen Woods knew that wasn't true. Life was hard and expecting anything else was foolishness. A bad end was her final destination. Her best days were gone.

Glancing up at the clock she saw it was nearly five and as if this thought had summoned it she heard their Plymouth pulling into the driveway. The old car needed work and likely wouldn't last too much longer.

The car door opened with a creak and then swung back with a heavy slam. Her daughter's steps clamped heavily up the stairs and Helen mentally prepared herself for the daily battle.

"Hey, Beverly," she said as the pretty dark-haired woman in the Brown Shoe Factory janitorial uniform opened the screen door and stepped inside. Helen noticed how worn down her daughter looked for a woman who was still a year shy of thirty.

"Hey, mom." The woman's eyes darted around the kitchen and her mouth opened as if to say something but instead walked through the adjacent hallway and back towards her room.

She's going to give me grief about not cleaning up and then ask what's for dinner, Helen thought. That was part of their arrangement. Beverly and Caleb got to stay with her and Helen prepared the meals. Beverly worked to pay the bills. For the most part it worked out.

"What's for dinner?" Beverly called out from her room where she was changing clothes.

Helen did a quick calculation of her food stocks. "Pork chops, mashed potatoes, and green beans. We still got half of that coffee cake left over for dessert."

No response. The old woman took another pull on her cigarette and imagined her daughter planning her next attack. It was hard to pinpoint when it had become like this. Hell, in her condition she couldn't be trusted to judge such things. Maybe it had always been like this.

Beverly walked into the kitchen and leaned against the fridge crossing her arms.

"Long day?" Helen asked.

"The usual," Beverly answered looking around at the kitchen. "I expected you to do a little cleaning today."

"Well, you know what they say about expectations," Helen said taking a sip of whiskey.

"What's that?"

Helen smiled at her. "They're the leading cause of disappointments."

"I guess you would know that better than most," Beverly said with a frown. "You been drinking all day?"

"No, just since breakfast," Helen lifted her chin defiantly. "Only got back from the honkytonk a few minutes ago."

"Right. Where's Caleb?"

Helen shrugged. "Don't know, he hasn't come home from school yet."

Beverly looked at the clock and frowned. "He's usually home by now."

"Don't be such a worrier. He's a teenage boy and it's nice outside. Probably off with friends playing baseball or something."

"He doesn't have any friends," Beverly answered looking out the kitchen window, "and the doctors have told him he's not supposed to play sports as you well know."

"It would probably do him good. Give him a chance to just be a kid. A mother can't protect her children from everything anyway."

Beverly turned on her with a tight face. "He's not like other kids, mom. He'll never be like the other kids. Caleb is a good boy, but he will always be slow. And he has to be careful with his condition, so he doesn't suffer any more damage to his brain. You know all of this. Are you intentionally bringing it up to hurt me?"

"I didn't bring it up," Helen answered, "you did. And the way he is isn't my fault."

"It's as much your fault as it is mine!" Beverly said her voice rising and tears forming in her eyes.

Helen prepared a responding salvo but held her tongue at the sound of heavy steps outside. The screen door opened and Caleb's frame momentarily blocked out the light. He slowly looked from one to other of them.

"How was school?" Beverly asked.

"Fine," he answered.

"Coming home a little later than normal," Beverly noted.

Caleb didn't respond for a few seconds. "Helped pick up trash on the playground after school for Mister Evans."

"That's nice," Beverly said smiling and touching his arm. "You hungry? Grandma will be fixing something soon," she looked at her mother when she said this.

Helen held up her mason jar towards Caleb. "Want a drink to hold you over till then?"

"Mom!" Beverly cried.

Caleb walked past them towards his room.

"I'm joking. He knows I'm only joking. Only person who doesn't understand jokes is you."

"No," Beverly hissed quietly. "He doesn't understand things. You can't expect him to. He's slow and it's almost like you're making fun of him."

Helen started to respond, but her daughter stomped away back into her bedroom. She sighed and mashed out her cigarette. "I suppose I should start fixing dinner."

Standing up she walked towards the counter and froze in confusion. "Now, what was I gonna fix?"

Then she remembered and smiled. Fried chicken, mashed potatoes, and peas. There was still some coffee cake for dessert.

Helen started humming a tune to herself as she began the meal.

Chapter 5

Denise Simms spent several days trying to build some level of trust with Caleb Woods. She encouraged him and was kind to him. She challenged him and urged him to participate more. She asked him questions and tried to solicit his opinion.

None of it worked. He was the same withdrawn and morose boy she had encountered on her first day. Denise was convinced Caleb was capable of much more. That despite what everyone thought, inside of this withdrawn lost boy was something special overlooked by the world.

But she couldn't do anything without Caleb. He had to meet her halfway. She couldn't do it for him. She had decided it was time to force the issue.

As the last class of the day was dismissed she stood in the doorway saying her farewells. She handed out warm smiles and encouraging words. When Caleb approached her to leave the classroom she stepped in front of him. "Take a seat, Caleb. I need to talk to you."

He stood there staring down at her while the other students piled up behind him. She smiled at him as sweetly as she could. Caleb stepped back into the classroom and resumed his normal seat.

Once the rest of the class exited, she turned to find him staring out the window with a look of intense sadness and longing. "Caleb, is there something I need to know about?"

He turned to stare at her but said nothing.

"Anything you want to tell me? Any concerns or problems you are having?"

"No, ma'am."

She sat down on the edge of a nearby desk. "You have not been completing the assignments. Not even making an effort. You don't participate or answer questions. It's almost as if you aren't really here at all."

He turned away from her to look out the window again.

"Do I need to get your parents involved? Might be a good idea to have them come down here so we can discuss the best way forward with you."

Caleb's gaze jerked back to her. "No."

"No, you don't want me to contact your parents?"

"No, ma'am."

"Then you are going to have to cooperate with me from now on," she said. "And that means completing your classwork, participating in class, and talking to me. Especially if you have questions or don't understand something."

He appeared to search for words before finally asking, "Why?"

Denise paused before answering. There were so many potential answers available. "Because you are capable of more. We both know that. I knew it the moment I saw your drawing."

His face turned slightly red as he turned away again this time to hide his deformity.

"It was beautiful," she said leaning towards him. "You are obviously talented. A natural artist. That means you have imagination, creativity, and observe the world around you. I think it means you are much smarter than you are letting everyone believe."

Caleb shook his head gripping the edge of the desk tightly.

"Perhaps I'm wrong," she said, "but we're going to start over. This time you are going to *try*. Otherwise, I'm going to call your parents. Do we have an agreement?"

He was looking her in the eyes now. Not defiantly, almost as if he were reassessing her. "Yes, ma'am," he finally answered.

"Good," she answered. "We're going to start now. You've not completed any of the assessment tests I've given you. These are important so I know your level in the school subjects." She pulled out a folder from her desk inbox and set it on his desk. "Start at the beginning."

Caleb sat immobile for a few seconds. He cast a longing gaze outside again before slowly opening up the folder and picking up a pencil.

Denise covered her mouth to hide a smile as he worked. She tried to pretend she was doing other tasks, but it was difficult not to watch him. It was such a sense of victory simply to have made this small connection with Caleb, even if there was a level of coercion involved. It couldn't be helped she told herself.

She noticed something curious while watching him. He appeared to struggle whenever reading was involved but worked through the other topic areas quickly after she explained the assignment. Of course, he could simply be rushing through in order to get out of school as fast as possible.

Denise also noticed that Caleb switched hands frequently while writing. Thinking back, she was sure he had used his left hand to make the sketch of her. Now he was using his right hand to write. She wondered if he used one hand for a little while and then switched to the other as it got tired. Studying him she spotted the moment when he passed the pencil to his left hand and kept writing. She stepped softly behind him and observed the area where he was having to write out his ABC's, both upper and lower case. He changed hands several times throughout this exercise, but she would not have known this from looking at the paper. Both right and left were the same.

Ambidextrous. This thought echoed in her head like an alarm bell. Her mind tried to grasp a thought, but it was just out of reach.

She noticed that he had stopped and was staring at the next assessment in front of him. It was a series of short reading assignments. "In this section you will read these out loud to me," she told him.

He stared at the page.

"Go on, Caleb. It's okay."

"Can you read them to me first?"

"Sure," Denise said with a smile. She liked it when the kids asked her for help. Leaning over the desk she read out, "The small brown beaver played in the stream all day long. The fish swam in the clear water. The birds sang in the trees."

Caleb leaned over and read, "The small brown beaver played in the stream all day long. The fish swam in the clear water. The birds sang in the trees."

"Very good!" Denise cried hugging him without thinking. He tensed and then slowly relaxed. "Now the next one."

Again, he asked her to read it first and she did. No matter how much she encouraged him, he would not read it without her reading it first. Her elation began to wane. She pointed at the word 'bird' from the first reading assignment.

"Caleb, what is this word?"

He hesitated. "Beaver?

"And this one?" She pointed at the word 'sang.'

A longer pause. "Trees?"

Denise picked up the folder and closed it. "Caleb, can you tell me what the first reading assignment said?"

Without hesitation he answered, "The small brown beaver played in the stream all day long. The fish swam in the clear water. The birds sang in the trees."

"And, what about the other reading assignments, can you remember them?"

He was able to recite all six from memory without error.

"That's very good, Caleb," she forced a smile. "We've got some work to do, but you've done very well."

He shifted in his seat and darted his eyes towards the window. "Can I go?"

"Yes," she said. "I will see you on Monday."

Caleb gathered his bag and stepped out the door and into the hallway.

Denise sat at her desk. She flipped open the folder and then closed it again. *Something isn't right. And I have no idea what I'm dealing with here.*

Again, she had the feeling that she was missing something. Something important just out of reach. Something that would connect all the dots that comprised the enigma that was Caleb Woods.

Chapter 6

Thomas was pleased with the progress he and Caleb had made. To be honest, Caleb did most of the work, but that didn't dim his sense of accomplishment. The gutters were cleaned out, some loose boards on the porch were tightened up, and the hedges were pruned for the first time in years.

"How you feel about painting?" he asked Caleb. The two were sitting on the porch with glasses of lemonade nearby.

Caleb shrugged without looking at him.

"Summer is the best time of the year for outdoor painting," Thomas continued. "In addition to the shed this porch could use a fresh coat. You hungry?"

"Sure," Caleb turned to him with sudden interest.

Thomas pushed himself up out of the chair with a groan. "I've got some leftover pork tenderloin from dinner last night. I'll make it into sandwiches. Hang on a minute. I'll be right back."

Stepping into the sudden dimness of his home it took a moment for his eyes to adjust. He paused in the hallway blinking. When they started to clear he saw the framed photograph of a beautiful young couple and a smiling little girl. Thomas' heart felt heavy whenever he thought of his little sister Candice and her husband Steve. And joyful little Jenny who used to sit on his lap and laugh at his stories. All gone now.

Without conscious thought his head turned towards Cairn State Prison. He imagined the man sitting in a cell.

"No, not today." Thomas forced himself into motion and towards the kitchen. "Too early in the day to dwell on dark thoughts." He pulled out the leftover tenderloin from the fridge and a couple of plates from the cabinet. Thomas made one sandwich for himself and two for his large, hard-working friend. He spread mayonnaise on his and started to ask Caleb how he wanted his sandwich but stopped. He decided to just fix it like his own. The young man looked like the sort who might become annoyed at having to make decisions on trivial matters.

As a gesture towards having something healthy he sliced up an apple and split it between the two plates before adding some potato chips. "That should do it," he said as he picked up the plates. He kicked the front screen door open and put the larger of the two plates in front of Caleb before sitting.

"Thanks." Caleb picked up a sandwich.

"Hang on." Thomas raised a finger. "First things first," he said and bowed his head. "Dear Lord, thank you for this food and your many blessings and provisions. Thank you for the work we have done today and sending me such a wonderful helper. Please bless Caleb and his family and forgive us all of our sins. Amen."

Thomas looked up to find Caleb looking at him. "You don't thank God for your food before meals?"

"Grandma does…sometimes," Caleb said taking a bite of the sandwich. He chewed with relish.

"Pretty good, right?" Thomas took a bite himself.

Caleb nodded and swallowed. "Who made it?"

"Well, I did, of course."

The boy looked at him skeptically. "Your wife didn't make it?"

"Never married, my young friend. I was a priest for nearly forty years, and the Catholic Church tends to frown upon that sort of thing."

"So, you had to fix all your own meals?" Caleb seemed to find this idea hard to digest.

"Yes, sad but true. In this cruel and unjust world, old bachelors have to either learn to prepare their own meals or they starve."

Caleb chewed staring off into the distance. "So, you're a priest?"

"Not anymore," Thomas sighed.

"Why not?"

Thomas took a drink of his lemonade and stared out over the yard. "The answer to that question is both complicated and simple. The simple version is that I no longer believed I was suited to serve in such a capacity."

"Why not?" Caleb asked again.

"What do you know about the Roman Catholic Church?"

"Grandma calls them mackerel eaters."

Thomas smiled. "An oldie but a goodie. I personally prefer salmon on Fridays if I have the option."

Caleb's forehead pinched in thought. "You stopped being a priest because you didn't like mackerel?"

The old man threw his head back and laughed. Chuckling he wiped his eyes. "No, that's not why. Mackerel eating is not a requirement."

"So...what?" Caleb asked around a bite of apple.

Thomas sat back and sighed. "My hypocrisy. There is no place for it as a priest. Do you know what hypocrisy is?"

The boy thought for a second. "Saying one thing and doing another."

"Close, but not quite right. A drug addict can know and say that drugs are bad but be unable to stop. No, a hypocrite is someone who says one thing and *believes* another. A hypocrite is a form of liar. Or...in my case, just someone who is weak and unworthy."

Caleb was frowning at him. He appeared to want to ask a question.

"It boils down to the fact that I can't forgive. Actually, that's probably not accurate. I don't *want* to forgive. Something terrible happened to my family. Something that can never be made right," Thomas said dropping his head. He was silent for a few moments before looking back to Caleb with a hint of anger. "I cannot in good faith preach of Christ's command to forgive yet refuse to forgive others myself."

The boy stared at him blankly.

"You don't understand, that's okay. Perhaps I'll tell you more one day. Does that at least answer your question?"

The boy shook his head.

"I'm afraid that's all the answers you're going to get today," Thomas folded his arms across his chest.

Caleb looked confused and opened his mouth again.

"Okay," Thomas said with a resigned sigh. "Ask your question."

"Where's your bathroom?" Caleb asked.

Thomas sat with his mouth open for a few heartbeats. "Down the hallway, first door on the right across from the kitchen."

Caleb stood and moved past him. Thomas sat for a few moments fighting to keep dark clouds of melancholy and pain away. He shook himself out of his mood and noticed that the boy's plate was clean. Thomas looked at his own and saw most of the food was still sitting there. He was no longer hungry.

Collecting the plates he walked inside and saw the boy standing in the hallway looking at something.

"That you?" Caleb asked pointing at a framed black and white photograph.

Thomas stepped behind him and saw a young cocky boy in boxing gloves. "Yes, that was me. Long time ago. I was one of the first golden gloves boxers under Arch Wald in Chicago. I was pretty good and might have tried my hand at being a professional, but God was already calling me by then. Still boxed some in seminary but not as seriously."

"I'm not supposed to fight," Caleb said looking at the old man and pointing at his own head sheepishly, "because of my defect."

Thomas nodded. "That makes sense. But not all fighting is done with fists. Most struggles involve your mind, your spirit or your heart. I hate to break it to you if no one else has, but this life is nothing but a series of fights. If you're not prepared to stand up and fight, then you won't respect yourself and no one else will either."

Caleb thought for a few moments. "I want to fight."

"Of course you do," Thomas said. "God is a warrior, and he made men to be warriors. To stand against evil and fight for good. That desire in your heart is a good one, just make sure any fight worth fighting is for the right reasons."

"To stand against evil and fight for good," Caleb said.

"Exactly!" Thomas clapped him on the back. "You're a quick study in addition to being a hard worker. Speaking of which, breaktime is over. Let's get back to work."

Caleb followed the old man outside with the shadow of a smile on his face.

Chapter 7

Beverly Woods tires crunched over the gravel of the Brown Shoe Factory parking lot as she departed. It was still early afternoon, but her hours had been cut again. That made three times in the last two weeks and money was already tight.

Her considerable stress only increased when the old Plymouth whined and then the gear caught with a jerk. "Damn it!" Bob Myer, the only mechanic she trusted, told her it would be at least three hundred dollars to fix the transmission. He also said it would only get worse until it was fixed. If she waited too long to fix it then the whole transmission would need to be replaced and she believed him. He said, "You don't even want to know how much that's gonna cost ya."

Trouble was she didn't have three hundred dollars. Between her meager pay and mom's social security they were barely paying bills and buying food.

Beverly didn't want to go home, not yet. Mom would just start a fight and hound her over losing hours. Imply it was her fault for not working harder or being nicer. Her mind had been wandering, and she noticed she was driving past the hospital. Speeding up a little, Beverly felt the usual sense of shame and sadness near this place. She typically tried to avoid routes around it even if it took her out of the way.

Thinking of the hospital made her think of her dead father…and Caleb.

Thinking of Caleb gave her an idea. She looked at her watch and saw that school would be letting out soon. Turning left at the next intersection she drove through residential neighborhoods filled with people sitting idly on front porches. Many were cutting their lawns. Something else she would need to do soon.

You could just teach Caleb how to run the mower like mom says. Her mind jumped to an image of blood and screams. Caleb sticking his hand or foot into the blades out of curiosity. No. She would continue to do the mowing, she decided with a shudder.

Teenagers were already streaming out of the school by the time she slipped into the short line of vehicles. Most kids this time of year walked to and from school like Caleb. Laughter and easy banter flew back and forth among happy children. Searching among the masses she finally saw Caleb.

He was easy to spot. Taller and bigger than most he moved purposefully. A small bubble of open space seemed to surround him with kids almost unconsciously keeping their distance from him. Beverly's heart ached to see the isolation he endured and hoped his simple mind protected him somewhat from that pain and rejection.

She stepped out of the car and called out, "Caleb! Caleb, over here!"

He stopped walking and turned to look in her direction. They locked eyes for a few seconds, and she had to wave him over. Finally, he started walking in her direction. Teenagers snickered and pointed at Caleb and her. Beverly stared back daggers at them all until her son reached their car and her face changed.

"Hey, Caleb. Let me give you a ride home from school. I got off work early."

The boy turned his head in the direction he had been walking and then back at her. "I want to walk. I have plans."

"Plans?" she spoke with a laugh. "What plans? Come on," she waved him towards the car. "You can do whatever it is you're planning later. Ride on home with your old mom."

He hesitated for a few more seconds before moving to the passenger side door, taking off his book bag, and getting inside. Once seated he stared straight ahead without expression.

She pulled away from the curb asking, "How was school?"

Caleb shrugged, "Fine."

An idea occurred to her. "I'm off early, I can fix dinner tonight instead of grandma. What do you think of that?"

"I like grandma's cooking."

"Me too," she paused, "for the most part. But it gets to be the same things over and over. Wouldn't you like something new?"

"Like what?" he asked suspiciously.

"Oh, I don't know. What would you like to have?"

He thought for a long moment. "Spaghetti."

"Good choice," she smiled. "I remember we used to eat that all the time. Haven't made it in a while."

"With garlic bread?" he asked hopefully.

"Absolutely," she answered. "We'll just need to swing by the store on the way home. I don't think we have any noodles."

Pulling into the IGA parking lot Beverly found a spot near the front. Turning off the car she hopped out and closed the door. She was already walking towards the store entrance when she noticed Caleb was still sitting in the car.

"Come on," she urged her voice rising.

"Can I stay in the car?" he asked.

Her mother's voice came unbidden into her head. *Good grief, Beverly, he's not a child anymore. Walks himself to and from school. You have to let him grow into a man and stop babying him.*

"No," she answered. "Come on in with me and keep your mom company."

He didn't argue. Caleb never argued. He was a good boy. Getting out of the car he closed the door and followed her. It was only then that she wondered if maybe he didn't want to go into public spaces because of his deformity. The way he looked different from everyone else had become something that she hardly noticed anymore.

Or tried not to notice. When she did it was hard not to be overcome with a thick heavy blanket of depression. Beverly hoped Caleb didn't obsess over how he looked. That wool hat he usually wore had recently disappeared. Which she was glad to see.

She led him past the produce and bread area to the aisle she knew contained pasta. Beverly's mind was already on the petty quips her mother would send her way on cooking. She prepared several comebacks and tested them in her imagination. As she turned onto the aisle she stopped dead in her tracks.

A small elderly woman with silver hair stood by a cart looking up at canned goods.

Stepping backwards, Beverly bumped into Caleb. Moving around him she turned to go in the opposite direction.

"It's there," Caleb said pointing to the spaghetti pasta on a shelf ten feet in front of them.

The silver-haired woman turned towards them. Her stern face and flinty-grey eyes assessed them both. A hint of understanding and recognition came over her face as she stared at Beverly.

Beverly wanted to run but her feet stuck fast. The old woman walked over and stood right in front of her. Beverly kept her head down.

"Beverly Woods. Is this him?" the old woman asked her face tense.

Slowly looking up, Beverly nodded. She saw the woman's stern appearance transform as she looked over to Caleb. Her tight face relaxed and a soft smile radiated. The hint of tears glinted in her eyes.

The woman lifted a hand to her mouth and kissed it. She then placed that hand on Caleb's cheek and looked as if she actually might break down and cry. Abruptly, the woman turned, grabbed her cart, and pushed it towards the end of the aisle and disappeared around the corner.

"Who was that?" Caleb asked.

"No one," Beverly answered and walked to grab a bag of pasta with shaking hands. "Let's go."

Caleb dutifully followed her through the checkout and back to their car.

Chapter 8

Thomas woke up gasping, his heart pounding heavily. His arm flailed out and knocked a glass of water off the nearby table onto the floor with a smash of shattered glass. He put a hand over his eyes and shuddered. Slowly he pushed the grey hair back off his forehead. The afternoon sun slanted through the windows and into the living room. Caleb hadn't stopped by after school, and Thomas realized he must have dozed off. He noticed that his back hurt from napping in his easy chair but that was nothing compared to the emotional turmoil crashing over him in waves.

It was that dream again. The bad one that had come and gone for over forty years. He was on the Bataan Death March once more. General MacArthur had fled in the middle of the night with his family leaving his outnumbered and overwhelmed troops to fight the Japanese in the dense tropical jungles of the Philippines. American and Filipino soldiers had held on for a brutal three months backed into the mountainous Bataan Peninsula until they ran out of food and ammunition. Seventy-six thousand starving troops racked with malaria and dysentery eventually surrendered to the Japanese. Captain Thomas McDaniel had been one of them.

At that point in the war, they didn't really understand how savagely brutal the Japanese could be. In the honor culture of Japan surrender was shameful and those who did so rather than fighting to the death or taking their own life were cowards undeserving of any basic human dignity or respect.

Their sadistic savagery knew no limits.

The near-dead survivors were force-marched sixty-five miles in tropical heat without food, water, or rest. Those who fell down or stopped were immediately bayonetted and left on the side of the path. As a chaplain, Thomas did his best to keep the spirits of those around him up, but the Japanese did not tolerate any communications between the prisoners. They especially did not tolerate western 'devil' religion. Despite this a number of good Catholic boys had gathered around him on the march. Just being together seemed to encourage and enable another moment of endurance.

Trucks filled with Japanese soldiers drove up and down the narrow road they marched on. Prisoners were forced to jump off into the jungle to avoid getting run over and then climb back into the road quickly and resume marching to avoid getting bayonetted. Many were unable to do so as evidenced by the bodies lining their path.

All of them were walking in a haze of exhaustion and sickness. Most everyone smelled of urine and feces as stops to use the bathroom were an instant death sentence. Hallucinations were common and Thomas could remember waking up from sleeping while walking. Waking and sleeping blended together into a strange nightmare reality.

The Japanese trucks did not bother to honk their horns. Many swerved intentionally to hit prisoners if they were close enough to the side of the road. Thomas remembered hearing a truck and stepping into the jungle brush without looking back. A truck rushed past him, and he felt a whiff of air by his head and looked up to see a

Japanese soldier in the midst of a backswing with a golf club. He had just missed Thomas' head.

The other soldiers laughed and ridiculed the man for his poor aim. He looked forward along the road to another target and saw a man shuffling along with his head down, his arms lifeless.

"Bennie," Thomas attempted to croak out a warning, but his voice was hardly more than a whisper. He drew in breath to try again just as the head of the golf club connected solidly with the back of Corporal Bennie Delay's skull. The good Catholic boy from Pittsburg crumpled over in a heap as the truckload of Japanese laughed and cheered into the distance.

Thomas shuffled up to the man pulling the rosary, Bible, and vial of holy oil from his pockets. There was a hole in the back of the man's head and clear fluid seeped out past the mass of brains.

Bennie had rolled over and was looking upwards. His eyes were already glazing over. They locked onto Thomas with a look of hope. The priest knelt near Bennie to administer last rites.

"Shi!" a rough voice yelled out, and Thomas turned to see a bayonet advancing towards him rapidly. He looked back into Bennie's pleading eyes as he heard the steps building up to a killing thrust.

Thomas stood and walked away from Bennie even as he felt the man's grasp on his pant leg.

The old man sat still for nearly a minute. If suicide hadn't been a mortal sin he might have taken that way out over the years. He climbed up out of his easy chair, turned and knelt on his knees and placed his head in his hands. "God, I'm sorry. I didn't have faith in you or your provision. You called me to minister to your flock and lay down my life if needed. I failed in both regards as you well know. Please forgive me and wash away my many sins."

Bennie's face came back to mind. The young man laughing and telling one of his many jokes. "Lord, please let him be in your loving arms now. Please don't let him be lost due to my weakness, my lack of courage and faith."

He thought of the Japanese soldier who had killed Bennie and his jaw tightened. "Lord you ask too much. You expect too much of this weak vessel. You know my struggles."

A verse came to mind. *For if you forgive others their trespasses, your Heavenly Father will also forgive you.*

"I know. I know, God," Thomas sighed. "I just don't seem to have it in me. Not yet at least. You forgave the unforgiveable and paid an enormous price to save us because of your incredible love for us. I know that and I know we are supposed to emulate your example. My heart is just not into forgiveness for those who don't ask and don't warrant it."

I will give you a new heart and put a new spirit in you. I will remove from you your heart of stone and give you a heart of flesh.

Thomas smiled and looked up. "Yes, Lord. I love and trust you, but as you said, 'the spirit is willing, but the body is weak.' You're going to have to do the heavy lifting on this one I'm afraid."

He laughed at himself and climbed stiffly to his feet. Using a dish towel, he cleaned up the water on the floor and then swept the remnants of the broken glass into a dustpan. Thomas walked into the bathroom and used a washcloth to wipe away the tracks of tears from his face. He straightened his shirt and pushed his hair into place. Looking at his watch, he saw it was near four o'clock.

"I guess Mister Caleb Woods is not coming today." He started to make a quip about the younger generation not having a work ethic or sense of commitment but kept his mouth shut. He doubted that such stereotypes applied to Caleb. He sensed there was something special about the boy. That God's hand was upon him.

Thomas said a quick prayer for the boy. He added a few for Caleb's family as well.

The old man decided he did not want to be alone right now. What he needed was some companionship to help him shake off the dark memories of long ago. He was an old hand at surrendering to shame and doubt that did no one any good. He considered self-pity a form of pride, and he had little to be proud of.

Taking his car keys off the peg by the door, Thomas stepped out into the warm summer light.

Chapter 9

Denise Simms sat outside the principal's office just like a recalcitrant student. Principal Brad Johnson wanted everyone to know he was very busy man so all discussions with him required appointments, and these were discouraged. Even when you had an appointment you were typically required to wait ten or fifteen minutes after the scheduled time.

Either he is incredibly disorganized, she thought, *or one of those arrogant types who believes his time is more valuable than others.*

Denise was not surprised that the secretary went to extreme lengths to avoid eye contact with her. The stern woman with a large curly perm and thick glasses also appeared very busy at appearing busy. Denise looked at the clock on the wall and caught the secretary smirking.

She had made the effort. Denise had been nice and polite. Attempted to join group discussions and even brought donuts for the teachers' lounge on several occasions. None of it mattered. Denise Simms was, and likely always would be in Cairn, an outsider.

The phone at the secretary's office rang and she promptly answered. "Yes, she's still here. Yes, sir, I will." She looked up at Denise grudgingly like all gatekeepers to persons of power, "You can go in now."

Standing, Denise took a deep breath. She walked to the door and after going in closed it gently behind her. "Principal Thomas, thank you so –"

"I can only give you a few minutes," he said. "Got to get out of here by four."

"Oh…okay," she stammered trying to recalculate her prepared speech.

He looked up at her. "We can always do this at a different time."

"No, hopefully this won't take long," she pointed to one of the two chairs across from his large desk. "Mind if I sit?"

The principal hesitated before giving a tiny nod.

She sat. "This is about Caleb Woods."

"The big, retarded boy? He giving you trouble?"

"No, no trouble," she answered. "And he's not retarded."

He waved a hand at her dismissively. "You know what I mean. Special education is an awkward term invented by those nosy ivy league types."

"No, that's not what I mean," she answered trying to get her footing. "I don't think he should be in special education at all."

He frowned at her. "Why?"

Denise took a deep breath. "He's artistic and ambidextrous. His memory is superb. He's a critical thinker. His reading ability has increased from first to sixth grade level."

"That's nothing to brag about," Thomas smiled condescendingly, "the boy's supposed to be in ninth grade."

"He's improved five grade levels in eight weeks. Also, his math is at an eighth-grade level. It would likely be higher if he were in regular classes."

The principal leaned forward with a concerned look. "Are you sure we're talking about the same boy? He's been retarded since he entered the school system.

Teachers spotted it early on. Simply look at his head for goodness sakes."

Denise resisted the inclination to get irritated. "They missed it because they didn't know what to look for. I believe Caleb actually suffers from dyslexia."

"Dyswhat?"

"It's technically a learning disability but not because they are not capable of learning. Dyslexics are highly intelligent, they simply acquire information differently and most have initial problems learning to read or do math. It's only recently been discovered. I attended a lecture about it in college."

"Uh-huh," he said. "Miss Simms, we're simple people down here and don't need you bringing your high-minded Yankee ways down here. We've done just fine."

"Yankee?" Denise said. "I'm from Wisconsin."

"Whatever. Caleb Woods is retarded as anyone can see by looking at the poor kid's head. I don't need anyone coming in here and trying to stir up trouble. Don't want to get that kid's hope's up."

"But he can learn," her voice rising. "He can have a normal life."

He sighed and sat back in his chair. "Even if he did have hysterexia, He –"

"Dyslexia."

"Whatever. What do you want to do about it?"

Denise leaned forward. "I propose we move him back into normal classes. Not at his grade level, or course, but perhaps into sixth grade for reading and maybe seventh or eighth grade for the other classes. Just until he catches up. He's a very fast learner and is willing to work under the right circumstances."

Brad Thomas was shaking his head. "That boy is way too big to be in classes with middle school boys and girls. He'd be picking on them or trying to grab the little girls' private parts."

"What?"

"It's out of the question," he looked at his watch. "Maybe you could refer him to a doctor. Perhaps there is a cure or a shot for this dysfixia."

"Dyslexia," she corrected saying the word slowly. "And its not that type of condition. It's a mental hurdle to overcome, but it can be overcome."

Principal Thomas stood forcing Denise to stand as well. "Miss Simms. As I explained very clearly when you were hired, your job is to do what you can with these *special education* students and keep them out of the way of teachers trying to educate normal students. Teach them to mind their elders and not flatulate in public and that will be good enough."

"But Principal Johnson –"

He frowned at her. "This meeting is over. I've been very patient and given you much more of my precious time than this topic deserves. If you want to continue to engage in this fantasy, then do it on your own time. But don't expect any more pay or relief from your other duties."

"That was never my –"

"Out!" He yelled pointing at the door.

Denise walked dejectedly out of the office past the smirking secretary.

Chapter 10

Thomas pulled into the small parking lot adjacent to the First Bank and Trust. He strode across the street watching for young, distracted drivers or old blind ones trying to kill him. The Cairn Veterans of Foreign Wars, or VFW for short, looked like a normal office building from the outside. Inside, for all intents and purposes, it was a bar.

Sure, they had meetings and did charitable work, but whoever said you couldn't conduct these activities in a bar. It was actually the primary purpose of the original British pubs, Thomas thought. Stepping inside he remembered why he didn't come here more often, the smoke. It hung in the air like a thick haze and the smell would adhere to his clothing like tar. Yet, he longed for the deep and unique camaraderie that could only be shared by men who had endured combat.

"Hey, Tom," said Jared Michaels who normally covered the bar during the week, "the usual?"

Thomas nodded. "Yes, please." He watched Jared fix his drink. Through conversations he knew the man had been a flamethrower man in the Pacific. One of the few to survive the war. The Japs hated them so much they would focus all efforts on killing those unlucky few who carried flamethrowers. He had won a silver star at Tarawa, but it meant nothing to him compared to losing most of his buddies.

He had once confided in Thomas late one night there at the bar. One of those nights that seemed to drag on forever when no one else was around. Jared said the dreams were the worst. "It took only seconds to burn up those Japs in real life. In my dreams it takes all night for them to die. Their screams nearly drive me crazy. I wake up and swear I can smell the burning flesh."

Another time Thomas had seen a big, grizzled drunk trying to sell a couple of Nazi daggers for whiskey money. A patron had made the mistake of saying there were lots of counterfeits out there now. The big man had grabbed him by his shirt collar and screamed into his face. "I know these aren't counterfeit because I watched the sons-of-bitches breathe their last dying breath before I took it off of them!"

Most of the men in the VFW had similar stories. Something haunted all of them. The VFW was a place where broken and mended men could gather and realize they weren't alone.

A short stocky man with a limp sat down a few stools from Thomas. "Haven't seen you in a while, padre."

"You know how it is, Malcolm," Thomas replied, "out doing the Lord's work."

Malcolm chuckled and took a long swallow of the beer Jared had set in front of him. He turned and stared at Thomas' drink pointedly. "It ain't none of my business, and I'm not judging," he pointed at the drink, "you sure that's a good idea? I mean with your…you know."

Thomas smiled and lifted up the drink. "Believe it or not I appreciate you being willing to say something." He took a sip of his clear bubbly drink. "It's just seltzer water."

The man's face scrunched up. "You like that stuff?"

"Not really. Kind of tastes what I imagine television static would taste like."

"Why you drink it then?"

"Well," Thomas paused for a second, "as you have alluded to, I have a love hate relationship with alcohol. I no longer partake but it doesn't mean I don't crave it or want everything that goes along with it. Nothing like a few years ago, of course."

"That's good," Malcolm laughed. "I heard some of those stories."

"I'm sure most people have." Thomas lifted up his drink. "If I close my eyes and don't think about it too hard it almost tastes like cheap beer."

The man threw back his head and laughed slapping the bar with his hand. He turned to the front door as it opened and the overhead bell tinkled. His laugh stopped immediately.

Kyle Trask walked in with Molly, his popular yellow lab. Many in the room cheered, calling the dog over with its wagging tail. Malcolm turned away and scowled.

"You don't like dogs?" Thomas asked.

The man answered without looking up from his beer. "I love 'em. Always have. I see dogs like that, and it always reminds me of Digger."

"Digger?"

Malcolm looked over at him. "My K-9 dog. I was a handler, in Germany. Best damn dog anyone could want."

"Something happen to him?"

"Yeah," Malcolm dropped his head. "I happened to him. Stupid asinine rules happened to him."

"I'm sorry," Thomas answered not sure what else to say.

"Thank you. Do you know that our dogs were trained to find Krauts by their unique smell?"

Thomas shook his head. "I didn't know that they had one."

"We can't smell it, but dogs sure as hell can. Their sense of smell is a hundred times stronger than ours. Digger could smell a German from a football field away no matter where they were hiding. If they didn't come out and surrender, I'd turn Digger loose on them. That always did the trick. Germans know what a guard dog can do to a person. That dog loved it. He was a good dog."

"So, what happened to him?"

"The war ended," Malcolm took a deep drink, finishing off his beer and signaling Jared for a refill. "The brass up at Corps said they were too dangerous to bring back to the U.S. or turn loose. I begged them to let me take that dog home with me, but they wouldn't hear of it. Wanted to turn him loose but I was afraid he'd kill some little German kid."

"They put Digger down," Thomas nearly whispered.

Malcolm shook his head. "They ordered all the handlers to put their *own* dogs down. Threatened us with court martial if we didn't." He sat for a second looking into his beer. "I can still see that dog looking up at me with such love and trust. Right before I put a bullet in his beautiful furry head."

"I'm so sorry," Thomas said.

The man wiped his eyes quickly. "Yeah, what are you going to do." He chugged the new beer down, his Adam's apple working. He then slid off the bar stool while pulling out his wallet. He left a five-dollar bill on the counter. "See you around, padre. Watch those bubbly waters."

He was almost to the door before he turned back. The man started at the yellow lab before looking at Thomas. "It wasn't the dogs that were too dangerous to bring home. It was us. I wish they had put a bullet in my head instead."

Malcolm turned and walked out the door before Thomas could say anything.

Chapter 11

Caleb sat and listened to the kids all complain about the chili mac. He thought it was pretty good and ate with gusto. In fact, most of the school lunches were good. Today the chili mac was accompanied by corn, apple sauce, a slice of bread, and chocolate milk.

After slopping up the last of the chili sauce with his bread, Caleb stood up and walked back to the food line. An ice cream cup was an extra ten cents. Normally he never had ice cream, but with the money he was earning from Mister McDaniel, that was no longer a problem. Caleb had eaten a chocolate swirl ice cream cup every day for the last month.

As he was returning to his seat he heard the familiar cruel laughter that he had become so familiar with over the years. He looked over to see the Buttheads, Vic, Gus, and Moose approach the small happy, but suddenly bewildered, boy with Downs Syndrome. Timmy Dorn. It was too far to hear exactly what was being said, but Caleb could tell it was dripping with meanness.

Without really thinking about what he was doing Caleb made his way over to the table. Vic was sitting across from little Timmy Dorn with Gus and Moose sitting menacingly on either side of the boy. Caleb startled them all by slipping into the bench seat beside Vic and across from the other three.

"Whoa, look at that," said Gus. "Two freaks for the price of one. Must be our lucky day."

Caleb pulled the top off his ice cream, pulled out the wooden spoon, and began to eat. Vic seemed uncertain being this close to Caleb.

"Maybe we'll take your ice cream there, freak," said Moose.

Smiling at him, Caleb licked the top of the ice cream cup and then offered it to him.

"Ew," recoiled Gus, "you trying to give us retard germs?"

"Why don't you tell us how you got the name Hammerhead," jeered Moose.

"Why don't you tell me how you got yours, Moose," answered Caleb. "Is it because your face looks like a moose's butt?"

Gus laughed in surprise. Moose looked confused.

Vic finally spoke. "Maybe you should get out of here before something happens, loser."

"Don't leave me," pleaded Billy. "They scare me."

"I'm not leaving," Caleb told the boy.

"Bad call, freak," said Gus.

"Don't' call me a freak!" Caleb screamed at him. The entire cafeteria went silent.

The art teacher, Mister Sheldon stood from the teacher's table and rushed over to them. "What's going on here?"

Vic stood and the other Buttheads followed his head. "No problem, just the retards spazzing out."

"Don't call them that," Mister Sheldon said sternly.

Vic opened his mouth to say something.

"Keep that mouth of yours shut, Victor Brown," the teacher pointed a finger at his face. "One more word out of you, and I'll give you a paddling you won't forget, I promise you."

The bully peered up and down at the slim teacher but evidently didn't like what he saw. He turned and walked away. Gus and Moose followed with confused looks as if the world had suddenly stopped spinning.

"You two okay?" the teacher asked.

"We're fine," Caleb answered eating his ice cream again.

"THANK YOU!" Billy said loudly to Mister Sheldon. "You're my second favorite teacher after Miss Simms. She's nice."

Mister Sheldon smiled at Billy. "Thank you, I don't get that too often." He nodded at Caleb and then turned to walk back to the teacher's table.

Caleb kept an eye on the Buttheads. They watched Mister Sheldon until the teacher sat back down. Then they slipped over a couple of tables and sat with Zach Collins, a little nerdy kid with a fake leg. Caution and fear were evident in the nerdy boy's face. Caleb's nostrils flared and he felt his fists clinching.

"You're my bestest friend," Billy told him earnestly. "Thank you."

Caleb almost choked. Looking at the boy he saw he was sincere. His face contained nothing but admiration and acceptance.

"Anytime," Caleb answered. "Hey, would you like some ice cream?"

"ICE CREAM!" Billy nearly yelled. "I love ice cream!"

"Hold on then," said Caleb heading back into the line. "I'll be right back."

***

Caleb looked up from his multiplication tables and saw the last bell was about to ring. He had discovered that math made sense. Math was rarely confusing. There was a right answer and an infinite number of wrong answers. Finding the right answer felt like discovering something wonderful.

The bell rang and everyone stood and started gathering their belongings.

"Caleb," Miss Simms called out, "hold on. Let me talk to you before you leave."

Inwardly groaning, Caleb sat back in his chair. He wanted to get to Mister McDaniel's house. The old man was supposed to show him how to change the oil in his car. He didn't like to keep Mister McDaniel waiting.

Once everyone had departed she came over and leaned against a nearby desk. She looked nervous. "How is the new homework I've given you going."

"It's fine," he said. "Just a lot of work."

She nodded. "That's true but I think you can handle it, Caleb. In fact, I think you could handle much more."

"How?"

Miss Simms opened her mouth and then closed it. She walked over to the classroom door and closed it before returning. "Caleb, do you know why you and the others are in this special class?"

"Because we're dummies," Caleb answered.

She sucked in her breath and sat back in shock. "You are not! None of you are! All of you are just different."

Caleb nodded. "Yes, we're different."

"The world doesn't understand or deal well with *different.* It *likes* sameness. Everything is structured for sameness. When something different comes along it is sometimes hard for people to understand. Everyone in this class is different. They learn differently, in different ways, and at different rates. But different doesn't mean less. It just means different."

"It feels like less."

"I know it does, but you are not less. As a matter of fact, I actually think you are gifted in a number of ways."

He looked at her skeptically.

"Your art for one," she said with a smile, "and your math which is advancing very well."

"My reading is not so good," he said and dropped his eyes.

"But you're improving very quickly," she said touching him on the shoulder. "And I think most of your trouble reading has nothing to do with your intelligence level."

"If I'm not a dummy why can't I read like the normal kids?"

"First of all, there are no normal kids, everyone is different. Second, I believe you are dyslexic. This means your brain processes information visually and through experiences. That is why you are such a good artist and have an incredible memory. Some of the smartest people in history have been dyslexic."

He gave her another skeptical look.

"Albert Einstein, Eleanor Roosevelt, and Leonardo da Vinci to name a few."

"Leonardo who?"

Miss Simms smiled. "We'll get to that, and other things, but the key is to improve your reading ability."

"How?"

She leaned back on the desk. "It's going to take a lot of work. I've been doing some research and it's all about repetition and re-wiring the brain. We'll need to spend time after school doing some drills. Also, from this point forward you need to be only right or left-handed. I recommend being right-handed since the world is mostly built for right-handed people."

"No."

She turned her head slightly as if she didn't hear him correctly. "No, what?"

"I like using both hands."

"I understand," she explained, "but part of the challenge dyslexics face is training their minds to process information from left to right across a page. You read individual words well now. It is the sequence of words that sometimes trips you up. It's what most dyslexics struggle with. They read from left to right and at the end of the sentence try to go back right to left. I've read that making ambidextrous dyslexics either right or left-handed works wonders in this regard."

Caleb shook his head. "I don't want to."

The teacher sighed. "Listen, you don't understand –"

"That's right," he said standing and grabbing his bag. "I don't understand and I never will because I'm just a dummy." He walked past her and threw open the classroom door.

"That's not true," she hollered out after him down the hall. "You're scared. It's okay. Also, no one is *just* anything. People are not that simple, and neither are you."

He pushed through the hallway doors and escaped outside trying to block out her voice.

Chapter 12

Thomas was washing away the grime in his kitchen sink from changing his car's oil. He heard Caleb come out of the hall bathroom where he had done the same. He expected the boy to walk into the kitchen. He turned the water off, grabbed a dishtowel to dry his hands and turned to find Caleb in his living room staring at the large bookshelf filled with books.

"You're quieter than normal today and that's saying something," Thomas said.

Caleb appeared not to hear him and continued to stare at the books. "You read all of 'em?"

"Most of them. Many I've read more than once."

"Did they help you?" the boy asked.

Thomas walked into the living room and stood beside Caleb looking at the books. "Yes. God Almighty saved me from unspeakable darkness, but these books helped me through some very difficult times. Perhaps he even put them in my path to help me. Good books are often like good friends."

"Would they help me?"

The old man turned to face Caleb. "Have a seat, let's talk." Once they were both seated he asked, "What's on your mind, son?"

"I don't read that good...that well, I mean."

"But you speak surprisingly well and I believe you think deeply. Have a good memory too. If there is a gap in your education, that can be rectified. It doesn't mean there is a gap in your abilities. Do you want to become a better reader?"

Caleb shrugged. "I don't know. My teacher says I have something called dyslexia. Makes it harder for me to learn to read."

"I don't know anything about that but if you're asking my opinion, I think reading is the second most important skill a person can have after the ability to think critically."

"Why?"

Thomas waved his hand at the bookshelf. "Because if you can read, you can teach yourself to do anything else on this earth. You are beholden to no one under the sun except God Himself. There are libraries filled with free knowledge on every topic or task you can imagine. All you have to do is read about it."

Caleb seemed to think for a minute. "Miss Simms says I have to give something up. Something that is…part of me, in order to read better."

"Let me ask you something. Do you trust Miss Simms?"

"I guess so."

"Do you think she wants the best for you?"

Caleb nodded.

Thomas smiled. "Then I think it's an easy decision. Any growth or improvement involves discomfort and sacrifice. The ability to read and teach yourself is worth that. You're nearly a man, and I don't know how your parents feel about it, but you're getting old enough to make your own decisions. Just realize that the monumental decisions that shape our lives don't seem monumental at the time. They are just day-to-day decisions like this one. So, ensure it's a decision you can live with and not one you'll regret twenty or fifty years from now."

"It's just my mom," Caleb said quietly.

"Excuse me?"

"You mentioned my parents. It's just my mom, grandma and me. I don't have a dad."

"What happened to him?"

The boy shrugged again. "Don't know. Don't even know who he is."

"I'm sorry," Thomas said. "It's hard growing up in this world as a man without a father to guide you. Just realize you are never alone, God is always with you and he loves you. If you forget everything this crazy old man ever tells you, please don't forget that."

Caleb simply nodded and looked back up at the books.

"Don't you need to get home?" Thomas asked looking at the antique wooden clock on the wall.

"No, not tonight. Mom got some extra work helping clean the old folks' home. Said she won't be home till late. Grandma is playing rummy with her old lady friends. They won't drop her off until after eight."

"Would you like to have dinner with me?" Thomas asked. "You can call your mom if you need to."

"I don't need to call her. What are you having?"

"Pot roast with potatoes, carrots, and onions. It's my mom's recipe. Don't insult my dear old, sainted mother by refusing to eat."

"Okay."

Thomas clapped his hands together. "Excellent. I'll need to get working on that." He looked around and saw the daily paper on the table. "Read through this. The newspaper is good practice. Come ask me to help with anything you don't understand, but most understanding comes through context and working it out on your own. Can you do that? At least try?"

"I guess so," answered Caleb opening up the paper and spreading it out on the coffee table.

Thomas turned on a radio in the kitchen and hummed along to the music while he fixed the meal and set the table.

Caleb realized he had never eaten at anyone's house before except his own. He had to fight down an irrational urge to run out the front door. Instead, he looked at the pictures on the paper and tried to make sense of the words. The words themselves were never the problem. It was when they all ran together and tried to become something larger that he struggled.

There were the typical problems in the middle east and threats of oil embargos he heard about nightly on the television. He read about local and state politics and a plan to put in a highway to connect Cairn with Lexington. Caleb skimmed past the sports section but pored over the weather page. He found it nearly beyond belief that the weather could be predicted from winds, air pressure, and temperature trends.

He flipped to a section labelled obituaries. The page was filled with older looking women and men. This didn't interest Caleb and he started to turn the page. He froze as he saw a face he recognized.

"That's the section I unfortunately check every day," Thomas said from behind him. "I'm not from here but still know plenty of people from church and the VFW. Seems like funerals are a weekly occurrence."

"Do you know her?" Caleb said pointing to a black and white photo of an older woman with piercing eyes and high cheekbones.

The old man leaned down and read over Caleb's shoulder. "Martha O'Neil, age eight-one. No, I don't know her. Died Tuesday night from a stroke. Says she was a neonatal nurse at the local hospital for thirty-six years.

Never married, no kids. Survived by a younger brother who is former Knott County Sheriff Jason O'Neil." Thomas stood still and quiet for a few moments. "I do know Sheriff O'Neil. He retired years ago. A good and fair man."

Caleb kept staring at the old woman's photo.

"Do *you* know her?" Thomas asked.

The boy told Thomas the story of the woman who approached him and his mother at the grocery store. How she had placed a kiss on his cheek with her hand.

"There's definitely a story there," the old man said. "Sounds like your mother knew who she was by her reaction. You hungry?"

Caleb nodded and stood, leaving the newspaper on the table.

They ate a pleasant meal with some light conversation but mostly filled with comfortable companionable silence. Caleb ate seconds and with encouragement managed thirds. Thomas cleared the table and then brought out a plate of chocolate-chip cookies.

"Hope you don't mind store bought," Thomas said. "I try to cook, but baking is beyond me."

"I like 'em," Caleb said from around a mouthful of cookies.

Thomas looked over his shoulder out the window. "Looks like it's a clear night. Have you ever looked through a telescope?"

Reaching for another cookie, Caleb shook his head.

"Grab a couple more cookies and follow me." The old man led him out through the kitchen and onto the back porch. He carefully picked up a three-foot long metal tube on a tripod and carried it out into the back yard and set it on a tall metal table.

"I don't like having to bend over to see," Thomas explained. "Having it up high like this saves my back." He pointed the telescope skyward and peered through the tube making minor adjustments. "Now this is an easy one." He moved away carefully. "Try not to touch anything, just look through the lens."

Caleb stepped over and peered. He saw the moon, but never like he had seen it before. It was bright and large. It had texture and shades of color. The boy looked at the moon with his naked eye several times and then back through the lens.

"Let me show you something else," Thomas said eagerly with a smile. He gazed up into the sky to get his bearings and then moved the telescope and adjusted the dial. "Take a look at that."

The boy moved over and peered into the telescope. He knew from pictures he had seen in school that he was looking at Saturn but not like he had imagined. A voice in his head yelled out with surprised joy, *it's real!* The colors were vibrant and the rings looked so delicate and gossamer, like a spider's web. Caleb stared at the majestic planet for a long time before finally lifting his head away. He found he was nearly overwhelmed by an unknown emotion. He simultaneously wanted to yell out in elation to the sky and also be reverently silent.

"The heavens proclaim the glory of God," Thomas said with a smile. "They remind us of his power and majesty."

Caleb opened his mouth to say something and then shook his head and was silent.

"Go ahead," the old man said, "it's okay."

"Why did God make me this way?" the boy asked turning to look at Thomas and pointing at his deformity.

The old man's face softened. "Son, God didn't make you this way. Sometimes bad things just happen."

"Why did he let this happen to me?"

Thomas shook his head. "I'm sorry. I don't know. All I know is that there is a God in heaven who sees you and hears you and loves you. God is on your side and wants the best for you."

Caleb nodded. "I don't think the world wants me here."

"You have no idea how right you are, but God wants you here. You are right where you are supposed to be."

The boy turned away angrily. "That's no answer. It's not fair."

Thomas grabbed Caleb's arm. "Look at me and hear me well."

He turned around grudgingly.

"There is no *fair* in this universe and praise God for that. Fair is what we want when it's in our favor but not when it isn't. Fair is an illusion we think we want but really don't. Fair is an excuse to blame others and not to struggle and strive and take responsibility. Every situation and experience in this vast universe throughout all of eternity is unique. Nothing is the same. How can *fair* possibly exist?"

Caleb was ready to explode. He froze suddenly, everything forgotten. A lightning bug had landed on the tip of his nose. He focused his eyes down and could see the small bug also examining him. Carefully, he lifted his hand up towards his nose and the bug climbed onto his finger. Then it lit up in brilliant color before flying away.

"Well, isn't that something," the old man said.

"I have to go home," Caleb turned away.

"Good night, son," Thomas said as he watched Caleb walk around the side of the house towards the street. "May God's blessing and favor be upon you," he said softly. He started to make the sign of the cross over the boy's retreating form and stopped.

Thomas was constantly having to remember that he was no longer a priest.

Chapter 13

Caleb walked slowly home occasionally looking up into the starry sky. Before he stepped on the first step to his home he heard the raised voices of his mother and grandmother. He did not want to go in there, but this was his home and he had nowhere else to go. Caleb also noticed that the car was not in the driveway.

"Don't you understand?" cried out his mother. "We don't have the money to fix it! If we can't come up with three hundred dollars to fix the car, I can't go to work, and we can't pay the bills!"

"Just calm down," grandma's voice was a little slurred. "You're always so dramatic about everything."

"You can't understand, because you're drunk again, Mom."

Grandma laughed. "I doubt I'd understand it any better if I was sober."

They both turned to look at him as he came in the door.

"Where the hell have you been!" his mother raged. "We've been worried sick."

"Don't yell at the boy," grandma says. "This is about the money, don't take it out on him."

Beverly Woods pointed a finger at her mother. "I won't take advice on how to raise children from *you*!"

Caleb walked past ignoring them as best he could. In his room he pulled the shoebox out from under the old blanket in the back of his closet and came back into the room. The yelling stopped as he dropped the shoebox on the table and flipped the lid off exposing piles of cash.

He had an urge to laugh at the looks both of them gave him.

"Where did you get this?" his mom asked. "Did you steal this?"

Grandma scoffed. "Caleb ain't no thief."

"I got it workin' after school. You said you need three hundred dollars to fix the car. That's almost four hundred dollars."

"Working? Where?" his mother reached out a tentative hand to the box.

"How do you know how much money is in there?" grandma asked.

"I counted it."

Grandma peered at him with a look that was much less tipsy than it had been a few minutes ago.

His mom grabbed his arm. "Who are you working for? What are they having you do?"

"Mister McDaniel," Caleb answered. "I help him out around his house after school and he pays me."

"Who?" his mother asked.

"Thomas McDaniel," grandma answered. "The Catholic priest who moved here after his sister and niece were murdered years ago. I've heard he keeps to himself mostly."

"What type of work around the house?" Beverly's eyes kept going back and forth between the money and her son.

"I helped change the oil in his car today. Painted his shed and porch. Cleaned out gutters. Picked up limbs. Cut the grass –"

Beverly gasped. "With an actual mower!"

Caleb nodded.

"You could have been killed! Those things are dangerous! How dare he force you to do such things without consulting me first."

Grandma shook her head. "So dramatic."

"You shut-up!" she screamed at her mother.

"Who was Martha O'Neil?" Caleb asked.

His mother clamped her mouth shut and became slightly pale. "Who told you that name?"

"I saw her in the newspaper. The obituaries. She was the woman at the grocery store. You knew each other."

"You read the newspaper?" Grandma interjected.

"She's no one," his mother looked away from him. "Just someone from a long time ago. Nothing worth talking about." She looked at the money again. "We can't accept this money. You have to give it back."

"No! I earned it!" Caleb cried.

"Beverly," his grandmother said softly. "Be reasonable. This is the answer to our problems. You can take Caleb's money and use it to get the car's transmission fixed. Are you okay with that, Caleb?"

He nodded.

His mother shook her head looking at her son with a stern expression. "You should have told me. I don't like you keeping things from me."

"Like you keep things from me?" he asked.

Beverly gasped in surprise and took a small step backwards. "I've never kept anything from you."

"Who's my father?"

Time seemed to stop as everything froze. Caleb would have sworn it took ten minutes for the secondhand on the kitchen clock to move once.

"Wha-what?" she stammered.

"My father," Caleb said. "Everyone else has one. What happened to my father?"

"It doesn't matter," his mother said running a hand back and forth through the cash.

Caleb felt his jaw tighten. "It *does* matter."

Beverly sighed and looked up at him with the beginnings of tears in her eyes. "All you need to know about him is that he's not here, never has been. That was his choice. He doesn't want any of us."

"What is this all about?" his grandma asked him. "What has gotten into you?"

He fumed for a few seconds. "Nothing." Caleb turned and walked back to his bedroom closing the door behind him. He could hear some hushed discussion from the other room but no more yelling.

Caleb flopped down on his bed and stared at the ceiling. He closed his eyes and in his mind saw the little lightning bug on his finger lighting up so brilliantly and beautifully.

Sitting up, he pulled his notebook out of his bag and began to sketch the image.

Chapter 14

Caleb got up the next morning to find his mother had already left and that the shoebox of money was gone. He suspected she had walked to the mechanic to try and get the work done as soon as possible. Part of him wondered if he would get any of the money back and decided he didn't really care as long as he had enough for ice cream at lunch. Simply getting paid for work somehow made him feel more substantial. Like he mattered.

Grandma was in her living room easy chair. A cup of coffee and a lit cigarette were nearby. She waved at him from the living room. "Have a good day, Caleb."

He hoped he would. He was grateful there wouldn't be any follow-up discussions this morning about last night.

There was moisture in the air, and the morning sunlight made the dew sparkle like the lightning bug from the night before. He liked mornings. When everything was fresh and new. Even the birds sounded happier, more hopeful. How was it possible for this world to be so wonderful and horrible at the same time.

The old man's words came to him unbidden. *There is a God in heaven who sees you and hears you and loves you. God is on your side and wants the best for you.*

He walked slowly and purposefully with his head down delaying his arrival at school as long as possible. Not for the first time he imagined how wonderful it would be to run away. Thanks to Mister McDaniel he knew it wasn't impossible to make money if he needed to. Then he visualized his mother's worried frightened face. It would hurt her.

The busy hum of voices and moving cars told him without looking up that he was close to the school. The magic of the morning was nearly gone, and he lifted his head resolved to endure another day.

"Hey, pegleg," said a familiar voice. "Hop along little darling."

Caleb's head swiveled to see the Buttheads following closely behind little nerdy Zach Collins. The small boy was doing his best to ignore them as he made his way across the wide-open grounds to the school's entrance. Zach's lack of a response seemed to agitate them. They gave him little shoves and slapped him on the back of the head. Moose was kicking at the boy's feet.

Possibly by chance he connected with the boy's prosthetic leg while it was planted in the ground. Zach fell over onto the ground, and his fake leg flew off in the opposite direction. The three boys stared in gleeful surprise before laughing. Gus walked over and picked up the leg and started swinging it around. The three stood over the boy taunting and laughing while Zach was obviously close to tears.

Caleb hadn't realized he was running until he stopped in the middle of them. "Give it back."

Surprised, they stepped back a little, allowing Caleb to walk over near the fallen boy.

"Butt out!" yelled Gus waving the leg around. "This ain't got nothing to do with you."

Vic's face was turning red. "I'm getting sick of Hammerhead sticking his nose where it don't belong." He made a nod to Moose who was standing behind Caleb.

Caleb felt a sharp blow to his lower back that took his breath away. Stumbling forward into Gus he grabbed a hold of the other boy's shirt. More blows to his back, shoulders, and head while Gus tried to push Caleb away from him.

"Fight! Fight!" kids started screaming and gathered around.

Elbowing backwards, Caleb connected with some part of Moose and he heard a grunt. He grabbed hold of Zach's prosthetic leg and held on with one hand while trying to fend off Vic's punches to his face.

"Stop it!" came a voice of authority from near the front of the school.

"Teachers coming," Gus gasped letting go of the leg. "Let's go Vic. One more ding and you'll be expelled."

"Come on," Vic told the other Buttheads while giving Caleb a look filled with promised menace. Then they melted into the other students.

Caleb stood there panting the leg dangling in his hand.

"Thank you," a small voice said from close by.

He looked down to see Zach leaning up on one elbow with the other hand extended. "Can I have that back, please?"

Caleb handed the boy his fake leg and watched with fascination as he strapped it on before climbing to his feet.

"You okay?" the boy asked.

Looking down at himself Caleb saw he was a little dusty. He reached up to wipe at his face and found a small trickle of blood. Nothing more. "I think so." Caleb picked up his book bag that had come off sometime during the fight and began walking towards the school entrance.

Zach fell into step beside him. "You really whipped 'em good!"

Caleb didn't answer. His mind was elsewhere.

"My name's Zach Collins. You're Caleb Woods, right?"

Nodding, Caleb's mind was replaying the incident. He must have been punched a half dozen times. Maybe more. To different parts of his body, even his head. Yet he was okay.

"Those guys are real jerks."

"Buttheads," Caleb said and again marveled that he was okay. His mother had always told him if he ever got into a fight, or played sports, or did anything even mildly dangerous he could get hurt. Probably die. Horribly and painfully.

Zach laughed. "Buttheads, yeah!"

"I have class," Caleb said reaching the school entrance.

"Yeah, thanks, see you later," Zach headed to his locker.

I'm okay, Caleb thought again in wonder reaching up to touch the bloody spot on his head. It had already stopped bleeding. *I'm not even hurt.*

What else could his mom be wrong about?

***

When the final bell rang, Caleb remained in his seat. The other students gathered their things and made their way towards the door.

"Bye, Caleb," said Timmy Dorn with a big honest smile. "You're my bestest friend."

Caleb nodded and did his best to smile back. Smiling was not something he had much experience with. It felt awkward and goofy.

As the last students left the room, Miss Simms turned and saw him sitting there. "Caleb are you okay?" she asked walking over to stand near him placing a hand on his shoulder.

"Okay, I'll do it," he said.

It took her a moment to realize what he was talking about. "Working with me? To improve your reading?"

He nodded. "And only use one hand."

"Just for a while," she reassured him. "Until you train your brain. Just try to only use your right hand for most things including writing and drawing."

"I'll try."

Miss Simms beamed. "Good. Very good." She went to her desk and came back with a length of white yarn. "Let me have your left hand, please."

He lifted it cautiously in her direction and she tied the string around his wrist.

"That is to remind you. When you are reading and you come to the end of a line, remember the string and go back to the left. This is supposed to work."

Caleb looked at the string skeptically.

"Want to try it out?" she asked excitedly.

He shrugged.

Walking over to her desk she picked up a thick book. "I went ahead and picked something out for you. It's a little advanced but I think you can handle it. You might even enjoy it."

Caleb looked at the cover. It showed a blue, white and green mountain with smoke coming out of the top. There was what looked like a very large bird flying nearby. He read the title. "The hoab…it?"

"The Hobbit," said Miss Simms, "by J.R.R. Tolkien. It's one of my favorites."

He opened the cover hesitantly and began to read.

Chapter 15

Thomas sat down in the confessional booth at Saint Matthew Church. Pulling the door closed behind him, he made the sign of the cross out of habit. A latticework partition slid open almost immediately and he could see the priest's shadowy profile.

The old man felt small and vulnerable as he often did in such times. "Bless me, Father, for I have sinned. It has been one week since my last confession."

Father Peter Quincy only nodded in acknowledgement.

"Since my last confession," Thomas began, "I have used profanity several times. I also became irritated when I was stuck behind a farm tractor on the way to the grocery store on Tuesday. I thought unfair and unchristian thoughts about this person I did not know who was only doing their job."

Father Quincy sat patiently. He knew from experience there was more.

Thomas sighed deeply. "And I harbor hate and unforgiveness in my heart towards the man who murdered my sister and niece."

"Have you felt these feelings more intensely or frequently as of late?" Quincy asked.

"Yes," Thomas nodded. "His parole hearing is soon. I can't imagine they will let him out, but I'll go to speak at his hearing as I have before."

"Why do you go? Must be very painful."

There was a long silence. "To speak for Candice and Jenny. I am the only one left who can."

"Do you think God wants you to forgive him?"

"Maybe, I don't know. God made allowances for this. I am the avenger of blood, the kinsman redeemer discussed throughout the Old Testament. Frank Osbourne is currently in a refuge and protected from my vengeance…but if he ever got out…"

"'Vengeance is mine,' says the Lord. That man will answer for what he has done and pay for it more severely than anything you could ever do to him. God commands us to forgive those who have wronged us just as He has forgiven us."

Thomas shook his head. "Even All Merciful God requires us to ask for forgiveness in order to grant it."

"Would you forgive Frank Osbourne if he asked for your forgiveness?"

"He wouldn't."

Quincy leaned in closer to the latticework. "I'm asking you what *you* would do."

"I don't know," Thomas lowered his head. "A sincere regret? A repentant heart would make it easier."

The priest sat back. "God can work miracles and he can change that man's heart. He can also change yours…if you will let Him."

The silence stretched out between them.

"Is there anything else?" Qunicy asked.

"No, Father," Thomas said softly. "This is all I can remember. I am deeply sorry for these and all my sins."

"For the profanity and unchristian thoughts, you will perform ten Hail Mary's and ten Our Father's. For the hate and unforgiveness in your heart your penance will be to pray for the salvation of Frank Osbourne's soul at least once a day."

Thomas' fist clenched and everything in him rebelled. He could see tiny Jenny's coffin going into the ground. A running image of their last horrific hours on earth flashed through his mind.

Are you my servant or are you his, a voice said in his head.

He slowly let out his breath and cleared his mind. His fists slowly unclenched. *I am yours, always.* "My God, with all my heart I am sorry for my sins and for offending and grieving you. I firmly intend," here he paused and cleared his throat, "with your help, to do penance, to sin no more, and to avoid what leads me into sin."

The priest made the sign of the cross in his direction. "May the Lord God Almighty bless and protect and watch over you. May He walk with you and guide you and show you His mercy all the days of your life, amen."

"Amen," echoed Thomas. He stood and opened the confessional door and stepped out into the light. Something he had always thought was fitting after confessions. He made his way slowly into the empty chapel and sat down in a pew. After a few minutes a young priest sat down beside him.

"How are you doing, Thomas?"

"Not bad, Peter. My back is giving me fits, but the Lord sent me a helper."

Peter nodded. "That is always good."

"That was a gut punch in there."

"You have a moral obligation to forgive that man as hard as it may be to do so."

Thomas shook his head. "Now you've gone off the path. You were on solid ground with forgiveness tied to Jesus' teachings. I do not, and never have, believed in moral obligations."

"What?" Peter turned with eyebrows raised.

He smiled grimly at the priest. "A world ruled by moral obligations has no room for kindness or generosity or selflessness. All of those actions would be obligations one performed out of duty. I've noticed that people typically use the term *moral obligation* to get others to act in a way that they want."

Peter nodded. "Okay, good point, but *you need* to forgive him. Ask God to help you."

"I have," Thomas answered. "You need to learn this. It's not something they teach in seminary. God is not moved by our need, that is what should move us. God is moved by our faith. That is what I'm working on most."

The younger man sat quietly digesting this thought. "You could be a priest again, you know. Would you want that?"

"I would," Thomas said in almost a whisper.

"Then you know you can still serve God. The Bible is filled with sinful and fallen people doing his will. You do not have to be perfect."

Thomas smiled. "I know that. My inability to live a sinless or perfect life is not what disqualifies me. If that were the case no one on this earth would qualify. What disqualifies me from serving as a priest of the Most High God is that I am no longer holy."

"What do you mean?"

"Holy. It's means consecrated to God. To commit to serve and put him first, no matter what. Since…that day…I haven't been holy. Our Lord tells us very clearly how to fight evil, and when I am thinking logically I know the Evil One is our true enemy. I believe Frank Osboune is at least a vessel of evil, but he is not the enemy. Still…" Thomas shook his head, "we are emotional creatures. Just the way God made us. I wish with all my heart that I could forgive him. But I wish more for him to die and go to hell."

Peter Quincy stared at him solemnly for a few seconds. "Then sadly, you and the devil want the same thing," the priest said standing. He walked back to the confessional as an older lady entered the front doors.

Are you my servant or are you his?

Chapter 16

The old Plymouth drove smooth and easy, the gears shifted so effortlessly it was difficult to notice the change. Beverly Woods was amazed at the way the car rode. The mechanic told her it was a blessing that the car broke down when it did, otherwise it would have been a complete loss if she had driven it much longer.

She glanced over at the passenger seat. A paper grocery sack was nestled there with the remainder of the money. *Caleb's money*, it still amazed her to think of. Sixty-seven dollars and thirty-two cents after paying for the car repairs.

Turning onto Olive Street she saw the house coming up on the left. It hadn't been hard to get an address. Most people in town knew about the ex-priest connected to one of the most horrific crimes in Cairn history. She felt sympathy for the man but pushed that down. He had endangered her son. The old man had put a child to work without getting permission from his only parent. When the flurry of potential accident scenes flashed through her mind it nearly took her breath away. Caleb bleeding. Caleb not breathing. Caleb blinded. Caleb dead.

"No," she said out loud while loosening her clenched hands on the steering wheel. "He's okay, just a close call."

Pulling into a white gravel driveway bordered by a neatly trimmed lawn, she turned off the ignition. Peering up through the windshield she studied the old Victorian two-story house with its wide front porch. Stepping out of the car, she grabbed the paper sack and closed the door. Beverly began marching towards the front door gathering her righteous anger and indignation around her like armor.

"Hello," came a voice from the porch shadows. "Can I help you?"

Startled, she froze and even took a tentative step backwards. "Are you Thomas McDaniel?"

"I am," he said climbing slowly to his feet and moving to the porch railing.

She held up the paper sack. "You gave my son this money."

He looked at the bag in confusion and then at her before realization and a smile bloomed on his face. "Caleb, you mean. You must be his mother."

"Oh, now you recognize he has a mother?"

The smile slowly faded. "Ma'am, have I done something to wrong you?"

"You endangered my boy!" she nearly screamed while shaking the bag of money at him. "Caleb is not like other kids! He could have been hurt! I'm his mother, you should have checked with me!"

Thomas stared at her for a few moments. "You're right. I'm sorry. I didn't think it through I guess. Being old you forget things are not like they were when you were a kid."

Beverly was thrown off stride by the apology. She had expected a heated back and forth with accusations and denials flying fast and furious. "You're damn right, I'm right." Lowering the bag to her side it suddenly felt far too heavy. She realized how tired she was.

"Please," he said waving a hand towards an open chair in the shade of the porch, "come join me. I'll get you some lemonade, just made it. Hold on a second." Without waiting for her response, he went inside.

Beverly was still standing in front of the porch when he returned with a glass in his hand. "Would you like me to bring the glass out there to you? We can talk in the yard just as easily, but I don't have any chairs out there and the sun is pretty brutal today."

Glancing back towards her car and the street, she was undecided. She realized she would rather be anywhere other than here. All she wanted was a hot bath and to put her feet up.

"Caleb is a fine young man," Thomas said. "You should be proud."

This phrase nearly knocked the wind out of her. *Fine young man. Man.* She suddenly realized that he would be a man soon. That was a terrifying thought. The world was so cruel and unfair. For someone like Caleb it was doubly so.

Climbing the porch stairs, she sat in the white wicker chair the old man indicated and Thomas sank down opposite her. She set the bag on the nearby table and reached out a hand towards the lemonade. Cool beads of water were condensing on the side of the glass.

"Miss Woods," Thomas said, "please believe me when I tell you it was never my intention to do anything behind your back. I simply presumed, wrongly I now know, that Caleb would let you know that he was working for me."

"How did that come about? Him working for you."

Thomas waved an arm towards the street out front. "He was walking home from school one day and I asked him to help me. He did and I offered to pay him for other jobs I had around here. This place was in much worse shape a few months ago, I can tell you."

"What else did he do for you?" she asked with a clipped tone.

The old man shook his head. "I don't understand."

Beverly touched the paper sack with a finger. "There was almost four hundred dollars in there. You mean to tell me you paid a teenage boy that much money just to help you with chores?"

"No. I paid that teenage boy the state legal minimum wage, with a bonus in there every now and then, to work hard and honestly. To have a good attitude. To do whatever job I give him without complaint. That's what I paid for and that's what I got."

"Whatever job you give him?" she asked. "You know Caleb is special, right? He's not like other boys."

"I know that very well," Thomas said.

"Then you know how easy it would be for him to get hurt," she had to hold down the beginning of a sob. "The doctors have told me any blow to his head could kill him."

Leaning back in his chair he looked out over the grass. "I'm sorry I didn't know that. I would never do anything to endanger Caleb."

Beverly nodded and reached out to take a sip of the lemonade. "I appreciate that and am glad you understand."

"I think I do."

"Good," Beverly pushed the sack of money on the table over towards him. "This is only part of the money. I'll have to pay you back the rest when I can."

Frowning, Thomas leaned forward. "I don't understand. Caleb earned that money. It's his…or yours if you decide so as his mother."

"I also don't want Caleb working for you anymore," she said standing and starting to walk away. "Please tell him you don't need him anymore."

"No."

Beverly was near the bottom of the stairs and stopped. She turned back to the old man. "What?"

"I said 'no,'" he had followed her to the top of the stairs. "I won't lie for you or anyone. If you want him to stop working here that is your right as a parent but I urge you to tell him the truth."

"Oh, make me the bad guy!" her voice rising.

"No good ever comes from lying."

This statement froze her. Did this old man somehow know her past? How could he? "Stop filling his head with ideas," she finally said.

"His head is already filled with ideas. Some of them are wonderful and beautiful. I believe Caleb is more than you think he is."

She pointed an angry finger in his direction. "This is none of your business! Stay out of it!"

"What are you afraid of, Miss Woods?"

Beverly wanted to scream at him but the kindness in his eyes cooled her emotions. "I worry about Caleb. All the time. Of something bad happening to him. Of someone hurting him."

"I'm sorry to tell you this, ma'am, but I can promise you all of those things are going to happen to your son no matter what you do. If not sooner than later. But I can also promise you I will do everything in my power to protect him and keep him from harm."

She found she was close to tears and didn't trust herself to speak.

"Please trust me," he said holding out the paper sack for her to take. "He's safe with me."

Slowly she reached out and took the sack from him. Climbing into the car she backed out of the gravel driveway.

Chapter 17

Caleb's pace slowed as he started to hear the carnival music. The Knott County Fair was always one of the largest events of the year. Caleb didn't know this from personal experience having never gone, but he had heard about it at school. Amazing rides, mysterious foods, games, and strange sights spoken of only in whispered wonder.

Mister McDaniel had given him the day off along with some 'pocket money' as he called it to go to the fair. The old man took it as a given that Caleb was eager to attend. Caleb was embarrassed to tell him he had never gone to the fair, that his mother would likely forbid it due to the danger. If she knew, that was. Mother was picking up more hours at the nursing home and wouldn't be home until late. Grandma seemed to care about, or be aware of, things, less and less these days.

Over the trees he could see the top of a Ferris wheel. Its lights contrasted with the orange of the setting sun. To the left cars were parking in neat lines on a grassy field. Caleb felt a mixture of anticipation and fear. He wished he had brought his sock cap, but it was too late now. For a moment he considered calling the whole thing off and just going back home.

The distinctive bray of a donkey floated through the trees. Caleb remembered he had heard about the petting zoo. He had never seen a donkey before.

His steps increased and he ignored the looks he always got. People never could decide if he was invisible or ghoulishly fascinating. He stepped into the short line and was soon in front of the ticket booth holding out his money. The bored carnival worker hardly gave Caleb a second glance. *Probably used to seeing freaks*, he thought.

Groups of teenagers huddled around lines to rides. Couples on dates could be seen at games of chance or food stands. Families with small children gravitated to the smaller rides and the animals. Caleb started walking in that direction.

He could see the donkey watching people. A lone tired horse walked in a circle with a small girl on her back. In the larger open area kids and their parents mingled around sheep, goats, ducks, and chickens.

The man in charge of the petting zoo gave him a double take when he went inside the fence but then decided Caleb was invisible and looked elsewhere. Same for the parents. The small children and animals were not concerned by his appearance. Caleb first walked over to the donkey, and they stared at each other for a few seconds. Then the animal stepped forward and nestled his hand.

"He wants you to feed him," a little girl's voice said from nearby.

Caleb looked down at a tiny blond girl wearing a yellow summer dress. She poured something out of a cup into her hand and held it out to him. He held out his hand, and she dumped in a small handful of pellets. Before he could really realize what was happening the donkey leaned forward and ate them out of his hand.

"You get the feed over there," she said pointing to worker who had avoided looking at him earlier. A nearby table had small paper cups set out and a sign nearby. *Animal Food, 10 Cents/Cup.*

"Thank you," Caleb said and smiled faintly at the girl who smiled more exuberantly back.

"Abby," came a tense woman's voice. "Get over here, now!"

Caleb didn't have to look at the voice to know it came from the girl's mother. Scared that the troll would eat her little daughter. He reached out and stroked the donkey's head. The animal seemed to enjoy that but kept poking around at his hands and pockets.

"Hold on little donkey," he said and returned with a cup of purchased pellets. Those were quickly gone and he bought more moving on to the sheep and goats. He found if he sat in one place the baby goats would all come gather around him. Caleb liked the way they climbed in his lap and nibbled at his ears.

A strange noise surprised him. It finally dawned on him that it was him laughing. He had laughed and it wasn't hideous. It was like other people's laughter.

He heard the Buttheads in the distance with some cruel taunting. *No, not like everyone's laughter*, he thought. Sitting contentedly, he let the animals converge on him and he ignored everything outside of his small slice of delight.

"Hey, big guy," said a gravelly voice, "why don't you move along and let the little kiddos have a turn?"

Caleb looked up to see the petting zoo attendant staring at him. Parents were around the edges keeping their kids from entering within a ten-foot radius of him and most of the zoo's animals. He fed the baby goats the last of his feed, gently lifted them off of him and stood to his feet. The goats put their paws on him and followed Caleb as he made his way outside of the fenced area. As he was walking away the donkey brayed at him again and he had an urge to bray back. He almost laughed again imagining himself making animal noises and starting a panicked stampede.

The crowds had increased in proportion to the approaching darkness. The sounds of bells, buzzers, delightful screams, and machinery filled the night. Caleb looked out over the people and the rides and the noise and found none of it appealing. Especially not after the baby goats.

The drumbeat of belittling laughter drew his attention. Definitely not something he wanted any part of.

Then he heard ever so faintly underneath someone crying. Caleb strode through the throngs of people towards a circular crowd of teenagers. Everyone was laughing and pointing towards the center. He pushed his way through them and found the Buttheads facing little nerdy Zach Collins. His face was covered in tears while the front of his shirt and pants were covered in vomit.

"Little baby puked on the ride," laughed Vic pointing.

"Probably pissed his pants, too," Gus added.

Moose had a finished candy cane stick he kept using to poke at the flinching boy.

"Stop," Caleb said. He hadn't spoken it very loudly but his voice cut through the laughter and taunting. Zach looked up at him with a gleam of hope in his eyes.

Vic sneered. "I see they let you out of the pen to come to the fair. Or maybe you escaped."

"We saw you over there with the other animals," Gus jeered as the crowd laughed.

Caleb motioned for Zach to follow him and turned away from the bullies. He heard steps and braced himself just as someone pushed him from behind. Caleb stepped forward and caught himself using the momentum to swing one fist back behind him.

He felt it connect solidly. Caleb turned to find Gus on the ground holding his face.

Moose roared and charged at him. Caleb dropped one foot back shoving forward with both hands into Moose's chest. Pent up rage and frustration exploded, and the other boy's feet went out from under him. He fell and landed on his back. Caleb stepped forward and stomped down on Moose's stomach.

"Look out!" yelled Zach.

Ducking, Caleb felt something brush past his head. Vic flew forward off balance his fist still raised. Caleb roared in fury and marched towards Vic.

Vic ran.

There was stunned silence. Caleb breathing hard looked around at the circle of faces and the two boys on the ground groaning. "Come on," he said to Zach and started walking into the crowd, not waiting for them to make way for him.

Marching through the throngs of people he could hear Zach jogging along behind them. *I fought them and I won*, he thought in wonder closely followed by, *I hope mom doesn't find out.*

"Where are we going?" Zach asked.

Caleb ignored him leading the boy to the men's bathrooms. He walked in holding the door until the smaller boy came inside. He then closed and locked the door. Caleb pulled the trash bag out of one of the trash cans and emptied the contents into another can.

"What are you doing?" the boy asked with growing alarm his eyes darting from Caleb to the locked door.

Caleb handed him the bag. "Take off your shirt and pants and put them in here. Then wash yourself off in the sink."

Zach didn't move, only looked at the large boy with suspicion.

"I'm not going to hurt you. Would you rather I wait outside?"

Zach nodded. "What am I supposed to wear home?"

Caleb pulled off his brown t-shirt and handed it over. On the smaller boy it would go nearly to his knees. He stepped outside and heard the door lock behind him. After a few minutes Zach emerged in Caleb's shirt carrying the trash bag with his vomit-soaked clothes.

"Thanks," Zach said looking down at the large shirt covering him. The prosthetic leg was visible under the shirt. He then glanced at his watch. "My dad is supposed to pick me up in about ten minutes, do you want a ride?"

"No…thanks," Caleb turned away. The cool night air felt good on his bare skin, and it must have to others as well. Several men and boys also had their shirts off.

He turned back once to see the small boy standing there in an oversized shirt with a bag in his hand. Looking all the world like a small child.

Zach Collins waved to him.

Caleb started walking home as the stars began to light up the sky.

***

The next morning a smiling Zach Collins was waiting outside the school's entrance. Beside him stood an attractive and dignified woman in an expensive looking dress. She held a brown folded up cloth in her hands.

Zach saw him and waved. The woman's eyes found his but didn't dart away in fear or disgust. There was a faint smile on her thin lips.

There was no getting around them. Caleb moved forward resolutely and stopped in front of them.

"Caleb, this is my mom. I told her about last night."

The woman took a step towards Caleb and held out what he saw was his shirt from last night. It appeared to have been laundered and folded.

He took the shirt from her. "Thank you, ma'am."

She leaned forward and looked up at him. Then she kissed him on the cheek and whispered in his ear. "Thank you."

When she pulled back she patted Caleb affectionately on the chest and he saw she had tears in her eyes.

Sniffing, she turned and hugged Zach. "Have a good day," she said before walking away.

Caleb watched her until she disappeared from his view in the nearby parking lot. When he finally walked into the school, Zach followed behind him.

Chapter 18

Caleb pictured the bouquet of flowers in his mind. He didn't need to look towards the front of the room. He carefully sketched the clear glass vase from the picture in his head. How the green leaves even in death carried the shadow of life.

"That's very good," said Mister Sheldon from behind him.

Caleb looked up and saw the art teacher nod at him.

"We never really see something in the world until we try to recreate it. Then we are forced to study it with all our being. You have an incredible eye for detail and loads of natural talent. I'm glad we could get you in here." He smiled again and moved on to the next student.

Caleb went back to sketching. He was glad he was here as well. It had been Miss Simms' doing, and he had heard the principal fought her on it, but somehow he was here. He was the only special education student in the class, but after initial awkwardness, none of the other students seemed to treat him differently. Art wasn't a class you were forced to take and every student in Mister Sheldon's class was there strictly for the art despite being made fun of by the jocks and cheerleaders.

The class bell rang. While the other students packed their things, Caleb finished the petal of the yellow rose he was working on. He then closed the portfolio folder Mister Sheldon had given him, packed up his bookbag, and proceeded to the cafeteria. Unlike the other students he carried his things with him. None of the special students had lockers. Caleb supposed it was because the teachers likely doubted they could remember a combination.

Corn dogs, mashed potatoes, and peach slices were for lunch. Caleb gathered his food and went to his normal table. Timmy Dorn was already sitting there and his face lit up at the sight of the bigger boy.

"Caleb, my bestest friend!" the boy said. "You want my peaches? I don't like 'em."

"Sure," answered Caleb and slid his tray over next to Timmy's so he could scoop them over. He heard snickering and turned to see Vic, Gus, and Moose giggling and looking in their direction. Caleb stared back at them as sternly as he could until they turned away. In the weeks following the carnival incident, the Buttheads had given Caleb angry looks from time to time but mostly avoided him.

Zach Collins sat down next to Timmy.

"Zach! My third bestest friend," the boy said with a giant smile.

"Third bestest?" Zach said. "I'm moving up. You better watch out, Caleb, or I'll take your spot. Be Timmy's bestest friend."

Timmy looked troubled by the idea and frowned. "No, Caleb is my bestest friend. You are my third bestest friend."

"You set him straight," Caleb said around a mouthful of potatoes.

"Can I have ice cream?" Timmy asked Caleb. "Please!"

Caleb dug into his pocket and counted out some change before handing it over to the boy. "Go ahead and get three so we each have one."

"THANK YOU!" said Timmy loudly and scrambled towards the food line.

Zach shook his head looking in Timmy's direction. "It's really kind of sad."

"What is?"

"You know…how Timmy is."

Caleb turned and looked back over his shoulder to see the boy nearly vibrating in anticipation of getting ice cream. He turned back. "It's not sad at all. I wish I was like him."

Zach's eyes got wide and then he started to smile hesitantly. "You're kidding, right?"

"No," Caleb took a bite of his corndog. "Timmy is almost always happy. If something makes him sad, it doesn't last for long. Never worries about anything. Loves everyone and takes it as a given that most people love him back." He chewed for a few seconds his eyes off in the distance. "That'd be really nice."

"That's the most I've ever heard you say." Zach started rubbing his leg with a slight grimace.

"What's wrong?"

The smaller boy shook his head. "Nothing. The cup for the prosthetic rubs my stump sometimes, especially if it gets a little sweaty."

"What happened to your leg?"

Zach looked up at him. "No one has ever asked me that before. Do you really want to know?"

Caleb nodded.

"You remember that big flood we had about eight years ago? The one that took out the bridge over Miller's creek?"

"Yeah." Caleb remembered the fear in his mother's voice and his grandmother's eyes as they watched the water slowly climb up the steps to their house.

"I was making the last few rounds with my dad. He's a doctor you know. Said he wanted to visit his critical patients one last time in case they got trapped by the flood."

"A doctor?" Caleb asked in surprise.

"Yeah. So, the water was starting to rise fast. We were wading across Main Street, and I stepped into a grating. My foot got hung up and we couldn't get it out even after taking my shoe off. The water kept rising and my dad would take breaths and then duck under the water to try and pull it loose. He did that over and over."

"Wow. Did the police come or anything?"

Zach shook his head. "My dad kept yelling out for help. A couple of men came over and tried to help pull me free, but it was no good. I wasn't really afraid until I saw how scared my dad was. I'd never seen him like that before."

"What happened?" Caleb asked. He could picture the rising water and the panic of Zach and his father.

The boy didn't answer for a long time. "He had no choice. The water was up to my chest by that point and rising fast. My dad had one of the nearby men hold his medical bag open. He put a tourniquet on my leg, gave me a sedative, and then he performed an emergency amputation."

Caleb stopped chewing. "Emergency amputation?"

Zach nodded. "My leg was pretty numb by then from the cold but even with the sedative I felt it. He had to keep ducking under the water with the bone saw. Finally, I passed out. Woke up later in the hospital."

"Holy cow," Caleb whispered.

Zach smiled. "Holy cow indeed."

There was silence for a while between them. Caleb cleared his throat. "Do you and your dad…I mean do you…"

"Have hard feeling about it? Resent him?"

Caleb nodded.

"No. He saved my life. My dad is great. I'm pretty sure he feels bad even now about what he had to do. I hate not having a leg but I'm pretty sure I'd hate being dead even more."

"I suppose so."

"What about you?" Zach asked nodding towards Caleb's head.

"Birth defect," Caleb said reaching up to touch his scars. "Born this way."

"Tough luck."

Caleb looked down at the boy's leg. "Tough luck."

Zach smiled. "Oh, I almost forgot. Mom's making chicken alfredo Saturday night. You want to come over?"

"For dinner?"

"No, to clean up afterwards. Of course, for dinner. Her chicken alfredo is great, you'll love it."

Caleb pictured the beautiful woman who had kissed him on the cheek. "Sure."

"Great, be there at five. I'll write down the address for you. Do you need us to come pick you up?"

"No, I'll walk."

"You don't even know where we live."

"It's okay," Caleb answered. "I like walking and the town's not that big."

"You got that right."

"ICE CREAM!" yelled out Timmy crashing back into his seat. "I got chocolate for everyone because it's the bestest kind."

The three of them ate their ice cream in comfortable silence.

Chapter 19

Helen Woods woke gasping. She had been lost again. The same dream. The dream of her in a massive dark house with thousands of rooms and corridors and mirrors. The mirrors were the worst. They showed her a reflection that was always different. It was always her, but sometimes as a child, sometimes as she might look as an old lady and everything in between. More than anything she wanted to escape this house of mirrors, but there was never any escape.

She sat up in her easy chair peering around the living room. "Must have dozed off." Walking into the kitchen she froze. Dishes were piled up in the sink. The floor obviously hadn't been swept in days. Helen looked at the kitchen clock. It was nearly four o-clock.

“Oh, dear lord,” she whispered. Reuben would be off work any minute now. If he came home and found the kitchen like this he would beat the snot out of her. Probably beat little Bev as well for good measure. Reuben Woods did not tolerate a dirty house.

Her hands were shaking as she began filling one side of the sink with hot water. She pulled out kitchen drawers. “Where the hell are the dishrags!”

Nearly running she went to the laundry room and found several clean dish rags and towels on the shelf near the water heater. Grabbing a handful, she jogged back towards the kitchen and stopped in the hallway.

Facing her was her grandmother’s antique wardrobe. It had supposedly been *her* mother’s and come across the mountains from Virginia. Helen wasn’t entirely buying this story, everyone’s antique furniture seemed to have some old pedigree, but she loved the wardrobe regardless.

Its front had a massive full-length mirror and some old lady that looked like her grandmother was staring back at her.

“Reuben’s dead,” she said out loud. “Died of a heart attack. He’ll never beat me again.”

This is one of those silver lining sort of things, she thought. *I'm old but not getting beat daily by my drunk of a husband.*

She put her hand over her closed eyes. "I was just confused there for a minute. I'm okay."

I'm getting like Alice, she thought and had to fight back tears as she visualized her sister's rambling confused frightened last days. "Not yet, I still have time. I'm not that bad yet."

Looking down she saw the rags in her hand and wondered what they were for. Then with a jerk she went into the kitchen and turned the water off just before it overflowed into the floor.

She didn't want to think about Reuben. It made her want to drink and if she started this early that would likely result in an epic fight with Beverly. It seemed like these days she and her daughter were either ignoring each other or shouting at each other. Just last night Beverly had come home early and started on her about the dirty kitchen.

Helen's eyes roamed around her. The kitchen. Her responsibility. Something a woman still healthy and capable would take care of.

She walked over to the sink and began washing and rinsing each dish before placing it in the drying rack. Once that was done she cleaned off the kitchen table and then swept the floor. Surveying her work, she liked what she saw. She took the next hour straightening, dusting, and sweeping the house. By the time she had finished cleaning the bathtub, sink, and toilet her muscles were starting to ache. Helen had nearly forgotten the feeling and kind of liked it.

"You're reaching the limits of your endurance, Helen old girl." She decided she would get a load of laundry going and then maybe think about starting dinner. Grabbing the clothes out of her hamper she next retrieved dirty clothing from Beverly's room. There was still some space left in the washer, so she went to Caleb's room. She hadn't bothered cleaning his room because he always kept it so neat on his own.

He was a good boy. Damn shame the way he had ended up. So many regrets. That was what killed you. The regrets piled up on your back until the weight of them simply crushed the life out of you.

She grabbed a pair of jeans, some socks, underwear and a couple of shirts out of Caleb's basket. Spotting the edge of a sock under the bed she got down on one knee slowly to reach under and grab it. Pulling out the sock she saw a couple of rectangular items in the shadows. Reaching back further, she pulled them out and laid them on the bed. The top item was so unexpected that it took her some time to identify it.

A book? She thought. *Why does Caleb have a book? He can hardly read street signs, poor boy.*

"The Hobbit," she said out loud. It wasn't a book she had ever heard of and opened the cover expecting to find it full of childlike comics. Instead, the thick book was filled with words. So many words. There was a piece of paper serving as a bookmark near the end of the book.

"It can't be," Helen said wondering if she was having one of her episodes. Imagining things that weren't there.

Opening the notebook, she found a picture of their house. It looked simple but cheerful. Flowers were in the yard and the sun shined down through clouds. It wasn't something a child would draw. It looked real. It looked like something a real artist would draw.

She flipped through the pages and saw accurate and beautiful drawings of animals, plants, even some people. Her hands stopped flipping at the next drawing. It showed an older woman sitting at a table looking up at a younger woman. Both were smiling and laughing at each other.

The resemblance was unmistakable. It was her and Beverly.

When had this happened? Had it ever happened? Did Caleb create this image?

A tear slid down her cheek and she pushed it away. She had always assumed that Caleb was too simple and feeble-minded to really understand what was going on around him. That he was like a small dog who liked the affectionate pats, cowered at the owner's anger, but for the most part didn't understand. Oblivious to the daily vitriol that poured forth between them. Helen's stomach sank and she felt even more shame and regret.

She looked down at the book and the drawings. If Caleb could read a book like this, and make art like what she had seen, what else was he capable of?

Pushing the notebook and novel back under the bed, she climbed to her feet, started laundry and thought about Caleb. She flipped through every memory or interaction she could remember. Was he feeble-minded or had they only treated him that way because the doctors and teachers had told them such?

Helen went to prepare dinner with a hurricane of thoughts swirling in her head.

Chapter 20

Thomas' thoughts wandered as the rain poured down on the porch roof. If Caleb weren't here he'd likely be napping in his living room chair, something he found himself doing more and more often.

"Careful now," Thomas said as Caleb's hand hovered over his bishop. "Remember to ask the five questions before you make a move. Do you remember them?"

Caleb's hand froze over the piece his eyes studying the board. "Are any of my pieces in danger? Are any of your pieces in danger? Are any of my pieces undefended? Are any of your pieces undefended? What is the best move?"

"Perfect." Thomas thought the boy had taken to chess surprisingly well. He had almost sent Caleb home when the rain started not having enough indoor work for the boy. Teaching him chess had been an impulse idea that appeared to be working out well.

"Also think about what I am going to do next," said Thomas tapping an index finger on one of his knights.

Caleb saw the threat that would come in a few moves and castled his king.

"Very good," smiled Thomas. He pushed a pawn instead and Caleb began to study the board again. "They used to say that chess was like life, but I have learned that is not true at all. In chess each side starts with the same amount of assets. Also, each side takes turns with their moves. And finally, there are rules that both sides agree to and must abide by. Life is not that simple."

"There is also only one opponent." Caleb slid a rook to an open file.

"True," Thomas realized he needed to pay attention if he didn't want the boy to threaten his queen. This was the fourth game they had played, and Caleb was improving at a dramatic rate. He grudgingly pulled his queen back a square. "How is the reading going?"

"Better." He pushed a pawn as well threatening to fork Thomas' opposing pawn and knight.

"What's your favorite book so far?"

"Only read two real books. *The Hobbit* and *Lord of the Rings*. Started *The Two Towers* last week."

"Tolkien." Thomas let his surprise show. "A strong Catholic and devout believer. If you pay attention he weaves in Godly truth to his stories. It's also pretty advanced for a new reader. I'm impressed. Who is the character that you identify with most?"

Caleb looked up from the board at Thomas and then away.

"It's okay, there's no right or wrong answer."

"Gollum," Caleb said softly.

"Interesting. Why do you identify with him most?"

"Because he's the monster. And he has to hide away from everyone who hates him."

Thomas nodded. "I guess I can see that but remember Gollum was once normal and happy. He became the monster when he turned from light and embraced darkness. Then gave up everything for temptation. He murdered his only friend to get the ring. Smeagol became Gollum from the inside out. You are not him."

Caleb slid a bishop to an open diagonal. "I guess so."

"Listen to me," Thomas reached over to touch the boy on his hand. "You are not a monster. Nothing could be further from the truth. You were made in the image of Almighty God. *You* are his masterpiece. Not the beautiful creation and creatures we see around us that I know you admire. Caleb Woods is God's masterpiece creation, and you are precious to him."

"My precious," Caleb said with a smile while pretending to caress a ring on his finger.

"Not like that," laughed Thomas and took an undefended pawn. "Be careful of undefended pieces."

Caleb moved eagerly. The pawn had opened up a diagonal and the boy's bishop took Thomas' undefended knight. "You, too."

The old man shook his head and chuckled.

Caleb's smile faded. "I'm not sure if I believe in God. I'm mad at him."

"Those are two separate things. You can't be mad at something you don't believe in. Which is it?"

He thought carefully before answering. "I'm mad at him."

"Good," Thomas smiled. "Tell him about it. Scream your anger and frustration at him to the heavens but keep talking to him."

"Why?"

"Because he's your true father and he loves you more than you can imagine. Understand that God can take your rejection, it saddens him, but he can take it. What breaks his heart is you never knowing how desperately and completely he loves you. He moved heaven and earth so that you can be with him and lead an eternal life filled with joy and peace and contentment. You may not have a father here, but you have a father in heaven who knows your name."

"What about you? Why aren't you a priest anymore? Is it because of what happened to your family?"

Thomas looked up at him sharply. "Who told you that?"

"My grandmother said something. That your niece and sister were murdered."

He didn't answer for a few moments. "Yes. That is why I am no longer a priest."

"Because God doesn't love you anymore?"

Thomas frowned. "No, of course not. Nothing can be further from the truth. Nothing can separate us from the love of God."

"What about your sister and niece? Did God love them?"

"Yes, he did...and does. They are with him now. And before you ask how God lets bad things happen to people he loves, realize that love requires choice and freewill. To prevent those he loves from doing bad things would make them slaves. God loves us too much to allow us to be slaves to him. We are his beloved children."

The boy sat back in his chair absorbing this. "What about the man who killed them. Does God love him? Even after all he has done?"

Thomas stared at the board. He reached out and knocked over his king. "You win. Go on home now, I need to rest."

Caleb's face showed confusion and hurt.

"I'm not mad at you," Thomas sighed. "Just experiencing painful memories...and painful realities." He walked over to the front door reaching inside and emerged with an umbrella. "Here, take this. You can bring it back on Monday."

The boy accepted the umbrella and opened it as he stepped out onto the porch and then into the rain.

"Caleb," Thomas said waiting for the boy to turn and look at him. "I sometimes get mad at God too."

He then turned to walk solemnly into his house closing the door behind him.

Chapter 21

Zach was right, his mom's chicken alfredo was amazing. Caleb had three large helpings with garlic bread before he thought politeness required a little more restraint. His mother had seemed happier and happier the more Caleb ate while Zach and his dad tried not to stare. Zach's little sister Samantha had done nothing but gaze at Caleb in fascination since he had entered their house.

Their very nice house. The nicest house Caleb had ever been inside of. Zach had shown him around while the meal was being prepared and the Collins apparently had a separate room for every conceivable purpose. Four bedrooms, two separate bathrooms, an office for his dad, a library, a dining room, a basement game room, a large living room *and* a den. Paintings of beautiful landscapes covered the walls, and Caleb bored Zach by spending an inordinate amount of time looking at them.

And everything was clean and neat. Everywhere.

"How did you get so big?" asked the little girl.

"Samantha!" scolded her mother.

"By eating like this," Caleb answered.

Samantha looked down at her half-finished plate. She tentatively picked up her fork and took another bite.

"Zach tells us you are a very good artist," Doctor Winston Collins said taking a sip of his wine.

Caleb turned to his friend in surprise.

"You are," Zach said eagerly. "I've seen what you draw."

"What do you draw?" Doctor Collins asked. "I love art," he said waving a hand at several paintings, "but I don't have an artistic bone in my body."

Caleb shrugged. "Animals mostly. And plants. Trees. Some people."

"I'd like to see what you have done," Doctor Collins said. "Next time you come please bring some of your art to show me."

Next time. The idea of coming to this nice house regularly was startling to Caleb. That they would want him back. He nodded in acknowledgement towards Zach's father.

He had a mental image of a near panicked Doctor Collins dunking under the rising flood waters to saw through his son's leg while Zach screamed and begged him to stop. It was nearly impossible.

"What happened to your head?" Samantha asked.

"Samantha!" cried out Mary Collins in embarrassment.

Doctor Collins held up a hand towards Caleb. "You don't have to answer her."

"Bear got me," Caleb told her. "Wasn't much older than you."

Her eyes widened. "Really?"

He nodded. "I was walking on the railroad tracks over by the grain silos."

"All by yourself?" she asked.

Caleb nodded. "I heard a horrible growling noise in the trees. I wasn't sure what it was. Then it charged at me out of the woods."

"What did you do?" Samantha cried out leaning towards him on the table.

"I thought about running, but bears are fast. They're too big and mean to fight. So, I laid down and played dead."

"Did it work?"

"Mostly," Caleb said pointing to his head. "Bear took one bite out of me and spit it back out before wandering off."

"Really?" asked Samantha looking behind her at the dark window.

"No," said Missus Collins. "He's just playing with you, aren't you Caleb?"

"Yes," he assured her. "There's no bears around here. They're all up north or out west. Only thing you have to worry about around here are angry squirrels."

"What do squirrels do when they get angry?" she asked her mouth halfway open.

"Bark at you and swish their tails," Caleb said seeing the squirrels in his imagination.

Samantha stared at him even harder until he finally smiled.

"It's a birth defect," Caleb told her touching his head self-consciously. "I was born this way."

"Wow," said Samantha her eyes even wider than before.

"Can we be excused?" Zach asked.

"Yes, you may," his mother answered. "I'll clear the table and we'll sit down for dessert in about a half hour. Caleb, do you like strawberry shortcake."

Caleb had no idea what strawberry shortcake was. He nodded. It was hard to imagine anything this woman prepared not being delicious.

He followed Zach to his room where he saw shelves of wonderful toys. He also had a chest filled with board games and puzzles. Zach told him his favorite games were Risk and Monopoly but those took too long to play and were better with more people.

"On family game nights we usually play one of those," Zach said. "Winner from the week before picks the game the next week, and I almost always win."

The idea of a family sitting down and playing a game together nearly took Caleb's breath away.

"Let's do Clue," Zach said setting the board up and explaining the game to Caleb. Zach then proceeded to win.

"What are you going to wear for Halloween to school?" Zach asked.

Caleb looked at him in confusion.

"Halloween," he said slowly. "Every year people dress up for school on Halloween."

"Nothing, I guess," Caleb answered.

Zach smiled. "I have an idea for both of us, just trust me. I'll help you put it together."

Mary Collins called them back in for dessert, and Caleb found his earlier assumption was correct. Everything Zach's mother made was great.

There was an easy and relaxed comfort at the table that Caleb found odd. The meals at his house were either nearly silent or filled with sparring between his mother and grandmother. Caleb typically ate as fast as he could to escape to his room. Here he felt he could sit and enjoy the talk all night long.

"I told Caleb about game night," Zach said.

"Yes, you should come," Missus Collins said.

Doctor Collins nodded. "That's a good idea. I need someone else to lose to besides Zach here."

"Thank you," answered Caleb more than a little surprised. "I'd love to." He looked at the large ornate grandfather clock in their dining room. "I should probably get home."

Zach's parents stood. "Thank you for coming, Caleb," said Missus Collins and she came over and gave him a hug.

Caleb hugged her back after a few seconds. He felt something cling to his thigh and looked down to see little Samantha hugging his leg.

"See ya, tomorrow," said Zach.

Caleb disentangled himself from Samantha and started walking towards the front door. "I'll see you out," said Doctor Collins who followed him out the front door.

Now he'll tell me to never come back, thought Caleb. *To stay away from his son.*

Out on the front sidewalk he stopped Caleb with his hand and they faced each other. Zach's dad looked at a loss for words and seemed to struggle before speaking. "Mary told me what you did for Zach. At the fair. You'll never know how much it means for someone to do something nice for your children until you have children of your own. Zach has had it hard."

Doctor Collins looked away, and Caleb wondered if he was thinking of the bone saw now.

"I just wanted to say, thank you and that you're welcome any time," he stuck his hand out.

Caleb slowly reached out his hand and shook it.

Doctor Collins then reached into his pocket and brought out a business card and handed it to Caleb. "I don't want to presume, but if you would like to come by my office I could take a look at that," he pointed towards Caleb's head. "We could do some x-rays. If you are mostly done growing I suspect we might be able to put in a steel plate under the skin. In a few months no one would even be able to notice."

The idea stunned Caleb. He tried to imagine himself in the mirror looking like everyone else. "We don't have much money."

He waved the idea away with his hand. "Don't worry about that. I'll talk to the hospital president. Don't think it will be a problem. Just call that number and make an appointment with my secretary. Also, be sure to tell your parents and make sure they're okay with it. You might even want to bring them with you."

Caleb nodded.

Doctor Collins shook his hand again and clapped him affectionately on the shoulder before turning and walking towards the front door. "Be safe getting home."

A curtain peeked back from the front bay window. Samantha waved to him, a stuffed horse in her other hand.

Caleb waved back and reluctantly began walking home.

Chapter 22

Caleb climbed the porch stairs to his house after spending the afternoon at Mister McDaniel's house. The old man had him put caulking and insulation around the doors and windows in preparation for winter. This made him wonder if this shouldn't be done at their own house.

He noticed that their car wasn't in the driveway and knew his mother must be working late again. In the kitchen he found his grandmother sitting at the table smoking, a cup of coffee nearby. At least it wasn't bourbon yet. She hadn't noticed him, and he watched her through the screen door as she stared off into the distance at nothing.

He studied her profile, the way he would study something he would sketch. Caleb noticed what he could only imagine was the accumulated stress, pain, and disappointment of close to seventy years. He realized if he could take all those things away, draw her as she could be, that his grandmother would be beautiful. Perhaps she had been one day.

"What do you see?" she asked without looking at him.

"Hi, grandma," Caleb headed inside past her towards his room.

"Sit down for a second," she said.

He paused before dropping his bookbag and sitting across from her. Both of them studied her hands.

"Been spending a lot of time with that old priest lately."

Caleb nodded.

"What do you do over there?"

Caleb told her about the chores and work around the old man's yard, garage, and house.

"He have you reading anymore newspapers?"

"Sometimes," he answered.

Finally, she looked at him. "You're not dumb at all are you?"

He shrugged and looked away.

She took a long drag on her cigarette and studied him. "I've seen the books you're reading."

He looked up at her sharply. "You went into my room?"

She nodded. "I've seen drawings too. You do those?"

"Yes ma'am."

Helen Woods sighed. "When did you learn to read so well?"

"Started a few months ago. My new teacher Miss Simms helps me."

"I'm sorry," she said reaching out to take his hand.

"Why?"

She pulled her hand back and shook her head ruefully. "For believing everything we've been told. For talking around you like you can't understand us. For not *seeing* you."

Caleb studied her face and decided she was beautiful once. He committed the face to memory to sketch later.

"You know we love you, don't' you?"

He nodded glancing away.

There was silence for several minutes before she spoke again mostly to herself. "You're becoming a man. It's hard to learn to be a man without a father. It snuck up on me, but it's not too late. My time is running out but I've still got some left. Having a good day today."

"Grandma?"

"Come on," she said standing and crushing her cigarette out in the ash tray. "Let's go for a little walk."

"Where?" he asked becoming slightly alarmed.

"You'll see," she answered with a sad smile. "It's time you knew the truth…at least part of it."

She locked the door behind them. They headed towards Main Street several blocks over. The sun was still warm but more pleasant and comforting than brutally hot like it had been for many months. Caleb realized this was one of the few times he could remember walking anywhere with his grandmother.

Her steps were deliberate and carefully considered. She looked up to greet neighbors who asked how she was. A quick witty comeback like, "I'm at the point in my life where I don't buy green bananas," or "Daylight savings time now gives me jetlag," were evidently practiced responses.

Once on Main Street they turned towards town. Shops were beginning to shut down for the day and traffic on the road was heavy. She stopped suddenly in front of

Bill's Automotive Shop. Caleb had noticed this place many times and wondered why mom never came here for car work. She always went to Bob Myer's place all the way across town.

They stood there for several seconds studying the mechanics finishing up for the day. The men in dirty coveralls were pulling cars in and out of the garage and cleaning up tools and sweeping the floors.

"There," Helen said nodding towards one of the men. "See him?"

Caleb saw a tall, big-boned man with dark hair and dirty hands. A lit cigarette hung out from the corner of his mouth. He was loudly talking to the other men lewdly about some woman he had seen that day.

His grandmother grabbed him by the elbow, and he looked down at her. "You wanted to know who your father is? Well there he is for better or worse. Andy Starks. A real cowardly no-good son-of-a-bitch if there ever was one."

Caleb watched the man for a while. His cruel smile and biting remarks to his coworkers reminded him of the Buttheads. On instinct he started towards the man.

Making his way across the lot he stopped a few feet away and stared at the big dark-haired man.

Andy Starks didn't notice him for a few seconds continuing on with his witticisms as he pretended to work. Finally, he saw Caleb out of the corner of his eye and looked at him in surprise.

"Better be careful, boy," he said with a mean stare. "Sneak up on a man like that you're asking to get your eye blacked for ya."

Caleb didn't say anything. He suddenly realized he had nothing to say to this man.

"What you want, freak?"

Caleb felt an urge to flee but the term freak put him back on familiar ground. He remembered what the old man had said about never looking away. About seeing them and making sure they knew you saw them.

He held the man's eyes, and he saw a hint of doubt appear.

"Come on, Caleb," grandma called out to him.

The man looked over at her and his smirking smile vanished. His eyes widened and he turned quickly back to Caleb as understanding came over his face. Then something that might have been fear came over him. He took a step backwards before turning and nearly jogged back into the garage interior.

Caleb walked back home with his grandmother in silence.

Chapter 23

"The usual?" Jared asked.

Thomas was tempted to have something stronger like he always was, but he nodded instead. Real drinking for him had always been a private affair anyway. Something he did late at night when the memories became nearly overwhelming. Being at the VFW was about companionship and an effort to hold off the drinking but he wasn't immune to the irony of the fact that he was in a bar.

It had been a hard night. In the dream he was back in Camp O'Donnell, the Japanese prison camp that was the end of the line for the Bataan Death March. They were all standing in formation, forbidden to move. The prison officers were walking down the line with their bare katanas, swinging them within a hair's breadth of prisoners. Anyone who moved was instantly beheaded.

Then he heard crying. Kneeling in front of the formation were Candice and Jenny. Grinning Japs held swords over their heads.

"Help us, Uncle Tommy!" little Jenny cried.

Thomas was frozen. He couldn't move a finger.

He managed to struggle up out of the dream gasping and sweating before the swords could completely finish dissecting his sister and niece.

Thomas knew he could pray for God to help him overcome these dreams. Yet he did not. He found it difficult to explain to himself but wanted the pain to remain fresh. So that he did not lose his focus on their murderer. The dreams were his reminder and perhaps part of his penance.

Jared returned with his seltzer water. "You hear about Malcolm Pence?"

"Who?"

"The guy you were talking to last time here. K-9 handler in Germany during the war."

"Oh, yeah," nodded Thomas. "What happened?"

Jared looked around before leaning close to Thomas. "Official word is that it was an accident but my cousin's a paramedic. Told me it was obviously suicide."

Thomas crossed himself and said a prayer for the man and his family. He remembered how Malcolm had left the VFW last time and wondered if he should have followed the man outside. Tried to talk to him.

"Blew his head off with a pistol," Jared said. "He's been by himself the last five years since his wife died of cancer. If I ever get to that point that's how I'll do it."

"Don't you dare!" Thomas said.

Jared leaned away startled at the old man's vehemence. "You going to tell me it's a mortal sin or something? I ain't Catholic, padre."

"It is a mortal sin whether you're Catholic or not," explained Thomas. "It is the final act of despair. Despair is the lie of the devil. There is always hope. This life is not all there is."

"You really believe there's a heaven and hell? After all we seen? You think any of us are getting into heaven after what we've *done*?"

"There is most definitely a heaven and a hell. We will all spend eternity in one of them. What we have done or not done on this earth does not determine our destination. Acceptance of Jesus Christ's salvation through his sacrifice determines our destination."

"That easy, huh?" asked Jared.

"Nothing about it was easy. What do you know about crucifixion?"

Jared shrugged. "Hanging on a cross, arms out. Eventually you die."

"There has never been a more painful or shameful way to die devised by man. Being burned alive, or dropped in hot oil, or impaled would all be mercies compared to crucifixion. It was not easy."

"Okay, okay," Jared held out his hands. "Regardless, heaven doesn't sound too great to me anyway. Singing and playing harps to God while floating in clouds."

Thomas smiled. "That is not what the Bible says heaven will be like. I'm sure we will sing and play music, but we will also explore, work, build, learn, and create. On a perfect new earth residing in a perfect new universe, all for us. We will be in perfect fellowship with everyone there. No doubt, no shame, no temptation, no pain, no sin, and best of all no death. Love and light will fill every fabric of our being. Time is no longer our enemy. We will do all that we were originally made to do."

"Originally made to do? How do we know what that is?"

"You probably won't, not until you get there, but God knows. If time or money or ability were not a constraint what would you want to do? Seriously, think about it."

The bartender took a sip of his whiskey. "I always wanted to make furniture. My grandad did that."

"Maybe you will then if…" Thomas held up a finger, "you have accepted God's salvation. Jesus says wide is the way to death, and many find it, whereas narrow is the way to life, and few find it."

Jared shook his head. "I don't think I'm one of the few."

"You could be."

"Padre, I burned people alive. Dozens, maybe hundreds of them. And I enjoyed it at the time. And I can tell you…I am not a good person."

"Good people don't get into heaven," Thomas explained. "Saved people get into heaven. Those who have submitted themselves to the god of the universe and accepted his free gift of salvation. There is nothing you can ever do good enough to earn your way into God's presence in heaven and there is nothing bad enough you could ever do to separate you from his love."

Jared looked around at the few patrons in the VFW sitting in far off booths. "How would I do that. Where would I even start? I'm so far from where I need to be."

"You're exactly where you need to be and you start where you are. All God requires of you is all that you got."

The bartender looked up towards the ceiling for a few moments and then nodded to himself. "Okay."

"Okay?"

"Yeah," Jared nodded.

Thomas took his hands and they prayed.

Chapter 24

Denise Simms was given the additional duty of 'Welcome Monitor' by Principal Johnson. She was required to be outside of the school welcoming students as they arrived and still be in her classroom by morning announcements. This was a new duty he had invented obviously to make her life more difficult and remind her that he was the boss. Other than being mildly annoying she did not mind very much. Sure, she had less time in the mornings when the students arrived, but she enjoyed greeting them.

Some even greeted her back.

Today was actually fun because most of the students were dressed up for Halloween. The costumes would likely be a distraction and prevent any classwork or learning, but it was only one day after all. Most of the girls were dressed as princesses and there were even a few

Princess Leah costumes from Star Wars. The movie had come out that summer and was all the rage. Boys were typically dressed as cowboys, soldiers, policemen, or monsters. There were a few astronauts and a Fonzi from Happy Days.

Denise made a mental note to dress up herself next year. She hadn't seen any of the other teachers in costume, but she thought her class would love it if she showed up as a clown or a pioneer woman.

She was mentally imagining her options when she started to hear laughter. It started out small and isolated but seemed to be growing. Turning towards the playground area she saw kids pointing and laughing as something unseen moved towards her. Finally, the crowd parted and she saw what everyone was looking at.

The first thing she spotted was a little pirate. He had a fake hook on his left hand and had a plastic curved sword and a toy flintlock pistol in his wide leather belt. A thick wide-brimmed hat hung over an eyepatch. And his boots were leather with the tops turned down. Correction. *Boot.*

Her smile faded in confusion. The little boy only had one boot, the other ended in a peg leg that he stepped quite easily on. *How can he do that?* She wondered if his foot was bent up behind him but that would be difficult to maintain.

Realization hit her all at once. This was Zachery Collins, the kid with a prosthetic leg. Her smile returned. What courage it must have taken for him to dress up like this. After years of trying to blend in and hide his handicap from everyone.

Denise's focus shifted as the pirate smiled back at his companion. Her breath caught in her throat.

Following behind the pirate was a large shark. It was wearing dark blue with a white t-shirt showing in the front. The book bag on the boy's back had a paper mache shark fin attached to it. But it was the boy's head that drew her attention. The lower part of his face was uncovered but starting at the eyes there was a large papier-mache mask with eye holes. It was dark blue as well. The mask broadened out into an open mouth with fearsome triangular teeth. Once it reached the crown of the head it opened up into two opposite flat branches with fake eyes on each end. The costume was a hammerhead shark.

It was Caleb Woods in the costume. The boy they called Hammerhead in meanness.

Caleb was looking around suspiciously with an angry demeanor, but this only made the kids laugh louder. They thought he was playing up the costume, acting like a hungry dangerous shark. Zachery pulled out his toy pistol and pretended to shoot at students, and many played along by acting like they had been hit.

Denise laughed with delight and Caleb's eyes found hers. She could see the caution and fear in his face even under the mask. She clapped and cheered at him. Caleb looked around as if realizing that the kids weren't actually laughing at him. The students cheered and laughed even more as the dangerous shark's head turned from side to side seeking its next victim.

Off to the side, Denise could see those derelicts Victor Brown, Gus Evans, and big Norm Nettles. They were doing all they could to boo the boys and belittle them with cruel comments, but the crowd drowned them out. The laughter and cheering were filled with happiness.

At the school entrance Zachery peered up at Caleb with a look that seemed to say, *I told you so.*

Caleb actually smiled back at him.

Chapter 25

Beverly Woods had pulled three double shifts in the last week and wanted nothing more than to put her feet up and go to bed early. These days it seemed like there was either too much work or not enough. Certainty was always in short supply.

She opened the back door softly in case her mother was napping. The last thing she wanted right now was a passive aggressive tennis match.

"There you are!" her mother screamed at her and threw something.

Beverly had barely enough time to duck before a glass shattered on the wall behind her. "Mom, what the hell!"

"I knew it! I found your underwear in my bed, my very own bed!" she screamed. "How dare you sleep with my husband under my own roof! How dare you!" She reached to grab the vase off the table.

Moving quickly, Beverly grabbed ahold of her mother squeezing her arms close to her side. The old woman fought with surprising strength. "Mom, it's me, your daughter, Beverly! Stop it!"

Helen tensed and then stopped fighting her. "Beverly? Is that you?"

"Yes," she let go of her mother. "Mom, what's wrong with you? Are you drunk?"

Her mother looked around in confusion and then sank into the kitchen chair panting. "No, just got confused, that's all." She put a hand over her face.

Beverly wanted to tear into her mother but saw she was shaking. "Who did you think I was?"

"Just some woman," her mother said sighing. "One of the many your father screwed around with."

Sitting down across from her mother she looked at the shattered glass on the floor. It would have to be cleaned up before Caleb got home or he might cut himself. Beverly turned back to face the older woman. "Mom, Dad's been dead almost fifteen years."

Her mother nodded, her hand still covering her face. “I know. Things just sometimes get confusing when you get old.”

“Not that confusing,” said Beverly looking back at the glass shards. “Perhaps you need to go see a doctor.”

“No!” her mother finally met her eyes. “No doctors. Don’t need them. I’m fine, just need my rest.”

Beverly looked at the wall clock. Her son would be home soon. “Can you get yourself together before Caleb gets home. This would all be too confusing for him.”

“I think he could handle it. In fact, I think he’s capable of far more than you realize.”

“What’s that supposed to mean?”

“It means that I don’t think he’s retarded like they have been saying all these years,” Helen explained. “I think they took one look at him as a baby with…with what happened to him and decided he must have brain damage. Everyone since then has just followed along.”

“Mom, you need to rest. You’re not thinking clearly.”

“I’ve seen the books he’s reading. I’ve seen his art. There’s more going on in that head of his than we believed.”

“Caleb doesn’t read.”

Her mom nodded. "Yes, he does. He said a teacher at school started teaching him. He's in a regular art class at school now. Perhaps you would know about this if you went to any of the parent teacher conferences that teacher Miss Simms keeps requesting."

"I can't take off work to hear once again how the best he can ever hope for is to dig ditches or lay asphalt the rest of his life."

"You're not hearing me, Beverly. Caleb is smart. At least smarter than we thought. He's growing up. We can't keep treating him like a little boy. Even the work he's been doing for that old priest proves that."

Beverly remembered the conversation she had with Thomas McDaniel. Her eyes wandered over to the spot on the table where Caleb had dropped the shoebox full of cash. The cash that had saved them.

Helen pulled out a cigarette, lit it and took a long draw. "I took Caleb to see his father the other day."

"What!" Beverly found herself on her feet with fists clenched.

"It's time he knew. He was going to find out eventually anyway, wasn't like it was a secret. Better to hear from us than some stranger."

"You had no right!" she pointed an angry finger in her mother's face. "That was my decision!"

"We both know how great all of your decisions work out, don't we?"

Beverly felt the blood drain from her face. "Don't you dare put that all on me. You know damn well you played your part in all of that. If you'd stood up to him for me things might be different."

"And if you'd stayed away from that boy like I said you would've graduated high school." Helen got the words out and then her face dropped.

Beverly turned to see Caleb standing outside the screen door. She wondered how long he had been there. "Caleb?"

He turned and walked away.

Chapter 26

Caleb sat quietly as the nurse flipped through a thick folder with a great many pieces of paper in it. The interior room was too hot and the lights too bright. Caleb hoped he wouldn't be there very long. He had already had x-rays, blood drawn, and had his blood pressure and heart rate checked.

"Doctor Collins will be in here in a minute," the nurse said. "You're obviously a very healthy young man which is impressive considering all you've been through."

He looked at her quizzically.

"It was my first year here when your mother came in. She was in bad shape. Nearly died delivering you. They thought you were dead especially after the doctor gave up, but Nurse O'Neil refused to let you die. They called you the miracle baby."

The door opened and Zach's father in a white lab coat stepped into the room. "Hello, Caleb," he said shaking the boy's hand.

The nurse handed him a thin folder, and he turned on a light-backed display on the wall and began slipping x-rays onto the screen. Caleb stared in fascination.

Doctor Collins pulled out a pen and used it to point at one of the x-rays. "As you can see right here the bones of the skull have grown in an inverted shape, obviously due to the…" he looked nervously at Caleb before continuing, "defect. The brain grew around that deformation, but Zach tells me you are quite clever so I would judge the damage to have been minimal. I'd need to refer you to a specialist to say for sure, but that is neither here nor there for what we are looking at today. The human body has an incredible ability to adapt and heal itself, especially when young."

He opened the thicker folder and began to flip through grunting to himself occasionally. Caleb could see his name was on the outside of the folder. Doctor Collins peeked over at him a few times while reading and seemed slightly nervous. Finally, he closed the folder and handed it back to the nurse.

"It looks like you're a prime candidate for a cranioplasty procedure. One of my colleagues would perform the operation but I believe you would see very promising results."

"What is cranioplasty?" Caleb asked.

Doctor Collins pointed back at the x-rays and pulled out his pen as a pointer again. "The procedure involves pulling a flap of skin back to expose the bones. Those bones are then either removed permanently or temporarily. I'd leave that up to my colleague to decide. Then a metal plate is installed in the same area to provide support. The bone fragments are then either replaced or discarded, and the skin is sown back on. The whole procedure should take a couple of hours, and I would expect full recovery in a few days. You'd need to take care of the stiches until they are removed, but otherwise it should be relatively simple."

"Will it hurt?"

"You'll be under anesthesia during the procedure and won't feel anything. Afterwards there will be some mild pain and discomfort. Possibly some headaches, but those will fade with time, and the pain medication will keep everything manageable."

Caleb studied the x-rays. He saw his skull in black and white with the bones in stark relief and the soft tissues showing up as shadows. On one side was a smooth surface that looked natural. The other contained a cratered divot that extended from his temple back behind his ear. "And it will make me look normal?"

Doctor Collins thought for a second. "It will make you look more like everyone else. Like you would have looked without the, uh…birth defect. The scars you currently have will remain, but this procedure should not make those worse and you can keep growing your hair to cover it up. Once its healed, most people won't have any idea."

Staring at the x-rays again Caleb visualized himself without that hated asymmetric shape. His eyes had studied the world around him and the beautiful things he could spot immediately. The ugly things as well. Caleb knew he was ugly, but more importantly he knew without a doubt that he wasn't *right*. That something was wrong. And Doctor Collins was talking about fixing that wrongness.

"Would I be able to play?" Caleb's voice caught and he had to steady himself. "Like the other kids?"

The doctor turned back to the x-rays. "You should be able to do that now. Although the bone is misshaped and indented, there is no brain exposure. You're safe to participate in sports and activities now."

Safe now. What else has my mother been wrong about? Always telling me what I can't *do.*

"Yes, I'd like to do it." Caleb said. "We can't pay though."

"It's okay," the doctor said turning to the nurse. "Hand me a parental consent form." He started writing. "You'll need to get your parents to sign off on this and then bring it back to schedule the procedure."

There was a perfunctory knock on the door before it opened and another nurse stuck her head in. "Doctor Collins you're needed in the ER right now."

He nodded at her. "Be right there." Doctor Collins handed the paper to the nurse. "Please finish filling this out for me."

"My mom has to agree to the surgery?" Caleb asked.

"Yes," the doctor said, "tell her to come see me if she has any questions or concerns. I can talk through them with her."

“Doctor Collins, it’s a Code Red,” came the voice from the hallway.

“Got to go,” he said and shook Caleb’s hand with a smile. “Don’t forget about game night at our house.” And then he was gone.

Caleb studied the x-rays again.

“You’re doing the right thing,” the nurse said writing on the form. “After all you’ve been through you deserve to live a normal life.” She flipped open the thick folder with his name on it a few times to consult some of the paperwork inside before writing again.

Caleb thought of the woman at the grocery store. The one in the newspaper obituary. “You said Nurse O’Neil’s name earlier.”

“Yes, she was the senior resident nurse when I first got here.” The woman smiled and looked off in memory. “The doctors can be such bullies sometimes, not Doctor Collins, of course, but she wouldn’t back down from what she thought was right. I remember her refusing to let them discard you. Martha O’Neil looked after you almost non-stop day and night for weeks in the baby unit. Nearly got her fired.”

He was quiet for a few moments. "No one ever told me that."

The nurse shrugged. "It's not surprising. Parents always want to protect their children from bad experiences. She probably doesn't even want to remember herself." She handed him the form. "Remember, get your mother's information and signature and then bring that back here for a pre-op consult and to schedule the procedure."

Caleb took the form and stood. The nurse smiled at him as he exited the hot stuffy room.

Chapter 27

Edwin Blake had been the Knott County Prosecutor for nearly thirty years. He probably could have been district judge if he had wanted to but the man had told Thomas several times that his calling was to keep wolves out of the pasture. He considered Knott County his pasture, the people there his sheep, and himself the watchful sheepdog.

Thomas liked and respected Edwin. He got to know the attorney well during the investigation into the murder of his sister and niece and the subsequent trial. The prosecutor had done everything in his power to send Frank Osborne to the electric chair. Instead, a technicality beyond his control had only gotten the murderer life in prison.

Edwin acted as Thomas' lawyer although he had never paid the man a penny. He had facilitated Thomas' testimony to the prison parole board encouraging them not to release the man. They had been through this twice before, and Thomas had expected much the same this time.

"Like I said on the phone," Edwin said leaning his large girth back in his office chair. "The testimony of the family's victim is not required at parole hearings nor is it protected by law. It is the warden's decision to allow or not allow."

"And you said there is a new warden?" Thomas asked.

Nodding, the lawyer referred to a note. "New guy is named Connor. He was appointed when Warden James retired a few months ago."

"Surely they won't grant him parole, even without my talking to them."

Edwin held his hands out to his side. "You never know. He was only convicted of manslaughter, and a life sentence is rare in those cases. The board may have sympathy for him given he has served over half of his original sentence. He also has a clean record inside. No issues or problems. Been a model inmate."

Thomas leaned forward and hissed through his teeth. "But he is a murderer."

"You don't have to tell me. Remember, I was there. I saw what he did and if it were up to me he'd already have ridden the lightning, but it's not up to me."

"I just can't believe it," Thomas shook his head. "What can we do?"

"I've written a letter to the board advocating in the strongest terms that they deny parole," Edwin said. "I suggest you do the same, but there is no guarantee the board will even read any letters much less take them into consideration."

"Would the law really let someone like him walk free? After all he did?"

"Absolutely," answered Edwin. "Remember the law is never about right and wrong. It's about that most arbitrary of ideals."

"Justice?"

Edwin shook his head. "Fairness."

"How is any of this fair?" Thomas said loudly and he had to keep reminding himself to keep his voice at a conversational level.

Edwin shrugged. "It's not fair from our perspective, but the law will see a man who is on a life sentence when ninety percent of those convicted of manslaughter only get fifteen to thirty. The board may decide he has been treated unfairly with the sentence compared to others of the same crime."

"This is just unbelievable. He should have been convicted of first-degree murder and gotten the death penalty."

"You're preaching to the choir, father. The bottom line is there isn't much we can do at this point. Don't stress yourself out yet when we have no idea how this will turn out. Who knows, there's a good chance they deny parole without us doing anything. I just want to prepare you in case this goes the other way."

Thomas sat hunched over with his head in his hands. "Do they realize if they let him out that whatever happens is on their heads?"

Edwin studied him for a few seconds. "Thomas, I know you're distraught right now at the idea of what could happen. Anyone would be. But…to not do anything, don't even consider doing anything, that would force me to prosecute *you*. That would not bring Candice or Jenny back."

Shaking his head, Thomas stood. He nodded to Edwin as he walked out of the prosecutor's courthouse office. He made his way down the dark marble floored hallway and out onto the front entrance. Stately columns rested on large granite blocks.

Suddenly his legs were weak, and he sat on the front steps to keep from falling. He felt light-headed and wished he were not there. That God had already called him home. That he was dead. This was too much.

Why God? he asked. *You are a god of justice. You punish the transgressions of the wicked. Your son said it would be better for a man to not be born than to do harm to a little child.*

Thomas remembered that he was supposed be saying daily prayers for the salvation of Frank Osborne's soul.

"To hell with that," he grumbled climbing to his feet. Once there he leaned against one of those columns and took in low, deep breaths. He thought of his sister, Candice, and how they had played together in the woods as kids. Little Jenny would be a grown woman by now, might have had kids of her own.

Lost. All lost. Because of the evil of one man.

Thomas' eyes roamed around at the strolling people, the cars on the street, the leaves blowing lightly in the wind. All of them clueless. His eyes settled on a blinking light. On. Off. On. It said Ray's Tavern and had beer and alcohol signs in the window.

"Why not?" Thomas grunted. Disregarding the traffic, he jaywalked across the busy street ignoring the screeching tires and angry car horns.

Chapter 28

So many books, Caleb thought as he walked through the Knott County Library. The only library he had ever been in was the high school library, and this made that little collection of books appear like a tugboat next to an ocean liner.

Walking among the vast shelves filled with tomes on every conceivable topic Caleb momentarily forgot why he was there. He remembered what the old man had told him about the importance of reading. That if a person could read they could teach themselves to do anything. For the first time he realized this might actually be true.

He had made his way to the non-fiction section and passed by shelves on auto repair, house maintenance, woodworking, sports, history, science, architecture, philosophy, and much more. He paused and flipped through a number of books in the art section showing works by the great masters. Sculptures in marble and vivid paintings in oil.

Walking down aisles he eventually found the medical section and was overwhelmed. Hundreds of books on a vast variety of topics. Caleb supposed a person could even teach themselves to bc a doctor if they read enough.

He opened up the piece of paper and looked at the information. Both the doctor and the nurse had acted oddly. Like there was something they were hiding from him. As if they were carefully picking their words.

The top of the form was standard information. Name, age, date of birth, place of birth, address. Beneath was a section under procedure where the nurse had written cranioplasty. Caleb pulled down a dozen or so books and took them to a nearby table to peruse. The one on cosmetic surgeries was the one he needed. The descriptions he found were in line with what the doctor had told him.

He returned the books and looked down at the form again. There was a block that stated purpose and after that the nurse had written – 'To repair in vitro cranial trauma.' It took him a little longer to find a book that explained that in vitro meant while he was in his mother's womb. Cranial trauma referred to something that had happened to him while he was there. Caleb also read about birth defects, and these didn't seem to overlap with anything that could be considered trauma.

Growing more confused he looked at the last line on the form. Out beside 'relevant prior medical history' she had written, 'Patient's mother reported with massive internal hemorrhaging in the last trimester of pregnancy. Patient's mother had undergone an unsuccessful late termination procedure, obviously not conducted by a medical professional. Patient's injuries were sustained during this procedure which likely involved non-medical invasive tools.'

Caleb read this part several times. He pulled several books but was largely unsuccessful in clearing up his confusion. At one point the librarian walked by and asked if he needed any assistance but he told her no. She looked at the medical books spread around him and then at his head and walked away with a look of pity on her face.

He found a book on pediatrics by chance and after some trial and error discovered that the index in the back allowed him to look up key words. These key words told him what pages to go to for more information.

The truth began to build slowly before hitting him suddenly. He had been skirting it for half an hour or more, his mind evidently not wanting to accept what it was reading. It was just too terrible.

He sat staring into space thinking about everything he could ever remember about his childhood. How his mother and grandmother had treated him. The strange looks and hesitancy of Doctor Collins and the nurse.

Unfortunately, it all made sense.

Caleb left the books spread out on the table and walked out of the library as if in a trance.

Chapter 29

Beverly walked into the kitchen and wrinkled up her face as the horrendous smell hit her. She recognized it immediately as it brought back painful and frightening memories. Her mother hovered over a steaming pan filled with liver and onions. No one liked liver and onions except her dead father.

"Mom, what in the world are you cooking?"

Helen turned to her. "Oh good, you're home. Can you set the table before your father gets home? It's Thursday you know and we always have liver and onions on Thursday."

"It's Tuesday," Beverly walked over to turn off the stove, "and dad has been dead almost fifteen years." She waved away the steam and moved the pan to a cold eye.

It would take days to get the horrible smell out of the house. She opened the windows over the sink.

Her mother looked around in confusion.

"Mom, you know we all hate liver and onions. Even you."

"Yes," she said softly. "I'm not sure what got into me. Just got a little fuzzy, I guess."

Beverly sighed. This was the last thing she needed after a difficult day. She had buffed all the floors that afternoon which would leave her lower back aching for days again. "Just throw it out and fix something else. I'm going to go change."

She was getting out of her work uniform when she heard heavy quick steps. Her door banged open suddenly. Covering herself up she turned to find her son standing there. He was panting and with his arms hanging before him, fists clinched.

"Caleb! You know you don't' come in my room without knocking! I'm changing clothes!"

He breathed deeply and glared at her darkly till she felt the faintest tinge of fear.

"How could you?" he asked. "All these years I blamed God. But it wasn't God who did this to me. It was my own mother."

"What are you talking about? Has everyone in this house gone crazy?"

"This!" he screamed at her slapping the deformed side of his head. "You did this to me!"

Beverly felt her stomach sink and sat down on the bed. "I don't know who's been telling you what, but it's not true. Just listen to –"

"It's true!" he screamed pulling a folded piece of paper from his pocket and shaking it at her. "You tried to kill me! Before I was even born!"

"No," she whispered. "I love you, Caleb. You're my son."

"Abortion! That's what they call it! And you couldn't even do it right!"

"You don't understand," she said holding her arms over her chest. "Please just let me explain."

"What don't I understand? How some dark alley hag tried to cut me up with a knife or a coat hanger? That's how the books say it's done. Or how you left me for dead at the hospital? What don't I understand?"

"I was so young," Beverly said softly as the tears flowed down her face. "My father –"

"You didn't want me," he hissed at her. "You've never wanted me."

"No," she whimpered shaking her head. "That's not true. I love you Caleb. I've always loved you. I made a terrible mistake. I'm so sorry."

"You're sorry?" He turned from her nodding to himself. "I guess that's supposed to make everything okay."

"I didn't know," she cried.

Caleb put his hands to his head and grasped double handfuls of hair. "I've been treated like a freak my entire life. Like an idiot. A broken toy the world can't bring itself to throw away."

"No," his mother said standing. She held her shirt against her chest to cover her partial nakedness. "I love you."

"How could you love me and do that?" he asked looking her over pitilessly.

"I'm sorry! I didn't know!" she sobbed.

He whirled slamming her door so hard it bounced back. She could see where the frame cracked.

"I didn't know, I didn't know, I didn't know," he said mockingly. "What was it that you didn't know?"

"That it was you!" she wailed. "I didn't know it was you!" She sank down on the bed burying her face in her hands.

She heard footsteps and peered up to see him shouldering himself past a confused Helen standing in the doorway. Then he turned and came back to stare at her.

"You are not my mother," he said deliberately. "I have no mother. I never want to see you again."

Then he was gone.

Chapter 30

Ray's Tavern was not like the VFW. The smell of spilt beer, old vomit, and violence hovered just under the surface. Walking in Thomas felt the darkness like old smoke, heavy in the air. Even the few low conversations were hushed and with sharp edges, hinting at violence. In the background twangy country music played lightly on the radio.

This was a place of scorn and despair. A gutter to gather those who had given up or given in.

"Don't just stand there, old timer," came a tired voice from behind the bar. "Either come in and close the door or go someplace else. This ain't no zoo."

A couple of patrons guffawed. Thomas stepped inside and closed the door. He stepped to the long, scarred bar and sat in a tall chair patched with duct tape.

A scraggly bartender with an unkempt beard and blond hair pulled back in a ponytail meandered reluctantly over. "Beer?"

Thomas shook his head. “Whiskey. Irish whiskey if you’ve got it.” He figured there was no point in fooling around. If you were going to fall off the wagon you might as well jump right off instead of letting it drag you down the road for a few miles. “Make it a double,” he told the bartender.

The blond man poured into a chipped glass and pushed it across to him. The bartender studied him for a few seconds as if trying to decide if he wanted a conversation with this stranger. Finally, he shrugged and walked to the far end of the bar to watch a game show on the small black and white television.

Reaching out with a slightly trembling hand, Thomas pulled the whiskey over to him. Putting his hands around it he sniffed in the wonderful aroma. It was definitely Irish whiskey. The perfect drink. A bite that got your attention but smooth enough to make you want more. He could already feel the warmth in his belly when it landed there. Anticipation of the mellowness that would come over him and make everything better brought a rueful grin to his face.

For a time, said a voice in his head. *The regrets come later.*

He dropped his head. *Lord, I'm done. I cannot take anymore, I'm sorry.* Thomas lifted the drink to his lips.

"Look at that would you," laughed a rough voice. "It's that freak boy!"

Thomas' hand froze and he turned to the window in time to see Caleb running down the street and then out of view. Something was definitely wrong.

He could really smell the whiskey now, almost taste it. The deep aroma tickled his nose, wanting to draw him in. Closing his eyes he absorbed that wonderful heavy flavor, but then he thought of the boy who had come into his life. The young man who had helped him.

Setting the drink down he walked to the door and out into the street ignoring the cries of the blond bartender. Turning to his left he could just see the backside of the boy before he turned up a side street.

"Caleb!" he cried out but his cracked voice was lost in the normal street noise.

Thomas tried to jog a little but just couldn't. *Lord, please protect that young man and help him. Let me find him and keep him from harm*, he prayed.

The side street led to another where Thomas saw no sign of Caleb. The far side of the street was bordered by trees and bushes that climbed a small hill and disappeared into darkness. There was a small path leading up, and he thought he saw a branch waving back and forth as if displaced by the wind. Or a passing boy.

Making his way carefully up the hill he heard Caleb before he saw him. There was a distressed moaning followed by sharp angry cries. Further up the path the bushes suddenly parted into an open clearing. Scenic hills stood off to the right and the Cairn State Penitentiary blighted the landscape off to the left. Thomas was surprised by the unexpected beauty of this little secluded grove. Then he saw Caleb.

The boy was on his knees leaning backwards his face towards the sky. His hands were on the side of his head as sobs shook his body.

"Caleb? What's wrong?"

The sobs cut off as if by a switch. He twisted to look at Thomas a moment then back at the sky. "I can't go home. Not ever again. I have no home."

Thomas walked over. "What's wrong?" He put his hand on the boy's shoulder. "Tell me what happened."

Ever so slowly, in fractured and heartbreaking pieces, Caleb did.

The old man stood there for a few moments. "I'm so sorry," he finally said.

"Yeah, me too," Caleb wiped his face with a shirt sleeve. "Nothing else? No lectures about God or forgiveness? How things all happening for a reason?"

"Not today," Thomas answered and put his hand under the boy's arm to help get him to his feet. "Come on home with me now."

The two trod side by side into the setting sun.

Chapter 31

Thomas closed the guest bedroom door softly. It had taken Caleb a while to relax and then even longer to try to sleep. Thomas had sprung for cheeseburgers and fries for each of them from Kilgore's, but the boy only picked at his food. As far as Thomas knew, this was a first for the voracious eater.

Caleb had finally asked for paper and a pencil, and the act of sketching seemed to calm him. Thomas saw amazing lifelike drawings of robins, groundhogs, deer, and a sprite-like woman who Thomas thought was Caleb's mother.

The boy cared nothing for chess, conversation or the telescope but seemed to be comforted by the old man's presence. Thomas sat in the bedroom until Caleb dozed off.

It was dark outside, and Thomas suspected Caleb's mother was worried. He had met the woman but never did get her first name. Pulling out the phonebook he was able to narrow it down to a half dozen "Woods" entries after eliminating those outside the city limits. He struck out on the first two calls, but the third one at least gave him something to work with. "Caleb Woods, that's Helen Woods' grandson. The boy and his mother Beverly live with her over on 6th Street." Thomas thanked them and ran his finger down the line of listings. He was able to locate the name and number.

"Hello," a hesitant voice answered after the fourth ring.

"Yes, is this Beverly Woods?" Thomas asked.

"No, this is Helen Woods, her mother. Who is calling?"

"This is Thomas McDaniel."

A long pause. "You're that old priest that Caleb's been working for."

"Pardon me for saying so, ma'am, but you don't sound like a spring chicken yourself."

"Fair enough, I suppose," she said. "Have you seen Caleb? He didn't come home tonight."

"That's why I was calling. I wanted you to know that he's safe at my house and he's sleeping now." He lowered his voice looking back towards the bedroom. "It's frankly none of my business, but I recommend you let him sleep here tonight and maybe try to talk to him tomorrow morning. He might be willing to see things in a different light then."

There was no answer. "Ma'am?"

"That's why Beverly's sad," Helen said almost to herself.

"Miss Woods, are you okay?"

"Yes, of course," she was suddenly very businesslike. "I appreciate you looking after him and we'll take care of this in the morning."

"Good night," Thomas hung up. He felt better having let the boy's family know he was safe. Now it was his duty to actually *keep* him safe. He resisted the urge to go sit by the boy's bed all night.

"He's in God's hands," he said to himself and then prayed for Caleb and his family.

The phone rang and Thomas picked it up quickly to keep from waking the boy. He expected to hear Beverly's voice imagining her wanting to talk to him after her mother told her that Caleb was okay. Instead, there was long silence.

"Hello?" he said again.

Nothing except heavy breathing. Perhaps even a suppressed sob. He was about to hang up when he heard a man's voice.

"They're letting him go." Deep heartache dripped down the telephone line like molasses.

"Who is this?" Thomas asked.

The man sighed. "They called me a while ago. Said I was on the list as the victim's next of kin."

"Steve?" Thomas asked. "Is that you?"

"How can they just let him go. After everything he did?"

Understanding struck Thomas and he nearly dropped the phone. The brother-in-law he had not heard from for nearly twenty years was telling him that the man who had murdered his wife and daughter was being paroled.

The man sniffed. "I keep thinking if I hadn't gone to visit my sick mother that night I'd have been there. Maybe I could have fought him off. Maybe he doesn't even break in if I'm at home."

"Steve, listen to me. None of it was your fault. You were a good father and husband," Thomas found he was close to tears now as well. "Candice loved you. Jenny adored you."

"What was it all for? I keep asking myself why it had to happen? No answers."

"Steve, where are you? Are you okay?"

Silence.

Thomas shifted the phone to his other ear. 'Steve, talk to me."

"Where is your god in all this?"

The line clicked dead.

Chapter 32

Caleb awoke in a strange room. It took a few moments to remember where he was. Then the dark reality crashed in on him again. *My mother didn't want me. It's an accident I'm even here.*

He started to pull the covers up over his head and go back to sleep but he heard voices downstairs. Mister McDaniel had never had anyone in his house other than Caleb that he knew of. Creeping down the hall he heard a voice he recognized.

"I think it's getting worse," his grandmother said. "I never know for sure what's real."

"None of us are getting out of here alive," Thomas told her. "We are all destined to die, the important thing is to know what comes next. I strongly suggest you're prepared."

She grunted. "You're talking about God and heaven and hell, aren't you?"

"I am indeed. I judge you are familiar with the concepts. Are you prepared?"

Silence. "I think so. I was baptized when I was twelve. A real baptism not some baby sprinkling like you Catholics do."

"Was your acceptance of salvation sincere at the time?"

More silence filled with consideration. "Yes. It seems so long ago now. So much has happened. I just don't know."

"Know that God has never moved away from you. He loves you deeply. If you are soon to be in his loving arms then I envy you. Just make sure that is where you are headed. There is nothing in this universe more important."

Caleb shifted his weight on the stairs causing them to creak loudly. He walked downwards as if he had not been listening. They were sitting together in the living room surrounded by books. Cups of coffee were on the table before them. The two turned up in his direction.

"Grandma," he said simply. "I'm not going back."

She nodded. "That's your choice I reckon, but I warn you it's a hard world out there for a young man with no place to go."

"I can stay with you, right?" Caleb asked Thomas.

The old man glanced back and forth between them. "Let's just take it one step at a time. We're not at that point yet, and I honestly haven't thought about it."

His grandmother waved Caleb over. "Come sit with us. I have some things I need to explain to you about what happened. It wasn't all your mother's fault, what happened to you. She wanted to come this morning. I convinced her not to."

"I don't want to hear it," Caleb said but sat down near his grandmother regardless.

She waved her hand at him dismissively. "It's not all about you. Perhaps I need to say what I need to say. I'm having a good day today. Not sure how many more of those I got in me, so I have to do this now. I've learned it's our secrets that entrap us, eat us up inside. Make us weak and vulnerable. I don't want you remembering me that way."

"I'll give you some privacy," Thomas said rising.

"No," said Helen. "Please stay. Consider this a form of confession if you will."

"I'm no longer a priest," Thomas reminded her. "Besides, the sacrament of confession is to God, not to me."

"Whatever," she responded. "All these rules remind me why I'm Methodist."

Caleb moved around the table and sat opposite his grandmother. She looked older and smaller than he remembered.

Helen turned to the scene out the front window. "I married Reuben Woods mainly to get away from my father. He was a brutal and mean drunk. Little did I know I was marrying the same sort of man I was trying to get away from. But…" she paused to search for words, "what we are used to can become comforting in a strange way, even if it is terrible. I grew up living in fear and then went right on living in fear when I married. From the time Reuben Woods died," she turned to Caleb, "shortly after you were born until now was the only time I didn't live in constant fear. That took a lot of getting used to. That was terrifying in its own way too."

She stared at him, her face stony. "I wasn't a good mother to your mom. I didn't think I could have children, had several miscarriages. Didn't have Bev until I was past forty. By that time Reuben had gotten set in his ways and used to the idea of not having any kids. Blamed me for not giving him the son he always wanted. Might have been different if she was born twenty years earlier. Anyway, Reuben was domineering and controlling. Everything had to be just right for him, and every transgression severely punished. That's difficult for a little child. It can sometimes take the light right out of their eyes." She examined her hands, rubbing at the wrinkles. "Beverly fortunately, or unfortunately, depending on how you look at it, was a fighter. She never openly defied him, but we could all sense it. That she didn't really submit to him. That she resented him. She rebelled, as many teenagers do. That drove him crazy, and he made her pay for it in all sorts of ways."

His grandmother took a slow sip of her coffee. She set the cup back down but didn't speak for a few moments as if searching for another way to delay what was coming. "When your mother got pregnant, I thought Reuben was going to kill her. Literally, kill her. He beat her black and blue with his belt and punched her all over. Reuben told her he'd never allow some bastard to live under his roof. That she had to get rid of it. By that point it was clear that Andy Starks was a worthless piece of…" she cut her eyes to the old man, "filth…and would never do the right thing. You have to remember she was only a little bit older than you when this happened. To be kicked out on the street as a single teen mother meant she would only have one option. To sell her body for money. She was terrified and alone."

Helen pulled out a pack of cigarettes and held them up questioningly towards Thomas.

"Go ahead," he said and got up to retrieve an ashtray from the kitchen.

She lit a cigarette and took a long draw blowing it out slowly. "I wish I could tell you I protected her. That I helped her, but I didn't. I was a coward. Maybe I still am. I can at least regret what I did and didn't do."

Caleb's grandmother stared at him intently. "I knew what your mother was going to do when her friend picked her up. She was supposed to spend the night with her, but I could see the tear streaks on her face. The devastation in her eyes. She was doing something she did not want to do but felt like there wasn't no choice." She took another drag on the cigarette and gazed out the window again. "She came home the next afternoon, pale, nearly catatonic, covered in blood, and without a baby in her belly.

"Everything at that point went back to some semblance of normal if you could call it that, but Beverly wasn't the same. The fight was gone. It seemed like the life had gone out of her. She was just going through the motions. It was about a month later that nurse from the hospital showed up, standing on our front steps with a baby in her arms."

"Martha O'Neil," Caleb said.

"Yes," she said looking at him curiously. His grandmother appeared as if she was going to ask him how he knew this but continued instead. "Reuben immediately started yelling at her and telling her to take that damn bastard baby somewhere else." Helen smiled now in memory. "That little lady stepped forward and stuck her finger in Reuben's chest. 'This is your grandson, Reuben Woods, and you're going to raise him and help take care of him. You're also not going to lay a hand on this baby or your daughter ever again.'"

"'Or what?' he had asked.'"

"'Or my brother the sheriff will pick you up and make sure you receive everything in return that you give out. I'll make sure he hurts you bad. You hear? My little brother dotes on me and does what he's told.'"

Helen smiled. "Reuben nearly lost his mind. Don't guess a woman had ever talked to him that way. She handed you off to Beverly. I can tell you I don't think I ever saw my daughter so happy. She was crying and laughing and immediately took you away."

Her smile faded. "Martha O'Neil then looked at me and told Reuben, 'I suppose a piece of filth like you can't help but beat something that can't hit back. If you have to hit something, beat on your wife here. She asked for it at least. Mind me though - not one hand on those other two. Not one harsh word or neglect. I'll know because I'll be checking in on them. Hear me well you lousy worthless excuse for a man.' Then she just left.

"Reuben followed out the front door, and I could tell he was about to scream something at her. But he froze. Sheriff Woods was outside our house leaning against his police car. The baton was already in his hand.

"He never did touch them again," Helen said, "just pretended they didn't exist and gave me all his attention. Within a year Reuben had a massive heart attack and died. That was one of the best days of my life." She mashed out her cigarette. "Since then, I can tell you your mother has worked her butt off every day to provide for you. She has done everything she knows how to protect you. She loves you, and she would do anything she could to take it all back. To make it better. To change things."

Caleb was leaning forward his head down.

Helen watched him for a moment and then nodded. "Guess I've said all I can say except, I wish you'd come home…and find it in your heart to forgive us." She put out her cigarette and carefully stood. She put out a hand as if to touch him on the shoulder but drew it back. Helen instead nodded to Thomas and made her way out the front door. Soon Caleb heard their old car start up in the driveway.

"Are you okay?" Thomas asked him.

Caleb shook his head. "What she said changes nothing."

"I think it changes everything. Your mother loves you and always has. She was in a horrible position and made a bad situation worse…but she was fifteen. Your mother did the best she could."

"How am I supposed to forget about all of this?" he asked the old man. "To just go back to the way things were as if nothing's changed?"

"Things can never go back to the way they were, but perhaps you can build something new. Something better. A relationship built on love and understanding rather than secrets."

"Love?" Caleb smirked. "How am I supposed to feel love for her after all this?"

"Love is not a feeling," Thomas said intensely. "Love is a decision. You can love her by deciding to love her, and I can tell you that love covers all pain, all transgressions, and all heartbreaks. Love is the most powerful force in the universe. And you have that power and potential within you."

Caleb stared at him for a few moments before standing. "I have to go."

"Where?"

"I don't know," the screen door slammed shut behind him as he left.

Chapter 33

Caleb went to school. He wasn't sure where else to go. Slipping in between classes it seemed like no one had even noticed he was absent.

I'm invisible, he thought. *No one would even notice if I ceased to exist.*

"Why is Caleb sad?" asked Timmy Dorn sitting across from him at lunch.

"I'm not sad," glowered Caleb taking a bite of baked beans.

"Yes, you are," Timmy said seriously. "It's not good to be sad."

"Why aren't *you* sad, Timmy?" Caleb asked angrily not expecting an answer.

The little boy smiled. "Because Jesus loves me. He makes me happy."

Caleb couldn't think of anything to say to that.

"Where have you been?" Zach Collins sat down with them.

Caleb picked up his tray and left them. The last thing he wanted was to talk to people. After dumping his trash and depositing his tray in the rack he walked out to the playground. Looking around he hoped to see the Buttheads. Getting into a fight with them right now seemed like the answer to everything. They were nowhere to be found, of course.

Sitting against a wall Caleb closed his eyes and felt the warmth on his face. In a few weeks it would get colder and he'd be raking leaves at Mister McDaniel's house. Caleb suddenly wished he had never discovered the truth. That his life had been simple and good without the painful knowledge he now carried.

Maybe that was the secret to Timmy Dorn's perpetual joy. He didn't know or understand the world around him.

Because Jesus loves me. He makes me happy.

The bell sounded and Caleb climbed to his feet. He went through the rest of his classes mostly in a daze trying not to think about the only thing he could think about. He worked with Miss Simms after class like usual. She complimented the progress he was making but his heart wasn't in it and perhaps she noticed because they ended early.

He sat in the wooded glade after school, but it no longer felt like the refuge from the world it had before. Nothing seemed beautiful enough to spend effort sketching. Caleb started towards Mister McDaniel's house but decided he wasn't ready for any more questions, spoken or unspoken.

Without really realizing how he had gotten there he was ringing the doorbell at the Collins' home. He was surprised to see Zach's father, Winston answer the door.

"Why hello, Caleb. How are you doing?"

"Is Zach here?"

Doctor Collins shook his head. "His mother took him and Samantha for ice cream. I couldn't go because I'm on call at the hospital. Have to stay near the telephone, just in case."

"Oh, okay," Caleb turned away.

"Caleb," the man's voice was more serious. "Are you okay?"

He nodded but was close to tears and then he felt a hand on his back.

"Come on in," Doctor Collins said. "I insist. You can wait for them."

Caleb allowed himself to be led inside and sat at the breakfast nook table staring out on their little garden. Zach's dad sat across from him.

"Now tell me what's wrong," the man said, "and don't say 'nothing.'"

It took a while to get started but Caleb realized he did want to talk. Perhaps he *needed* to talk. Bit by bit it all came out. When he was done, he somehow felt better.

"I'm so sorry," Doctor Collins said. "I can't believe she wrote all of that on the form. Should have never happened. I'll have a talk with her, you can count on that."

Caleb remembered the nurse being nice to him and didn't want her to get in trouble. "It's okay. She didn't know."

"She *should* have known," the man insisted. "But be that as it may, I'm sorry you found out that way. There's probably no good way to find something like that out but that was definitely not the right way." Doctor Collins peered at him for a few seconds. "What are you going to do about it?"

"What do you mean?"

"Well, it's not really any of my business, but I've gotten to know you over the last few months, and I believe you are a good young man. So, I hate to see anything that might send you down a bad path. Do you understand?"

Caleb nodded.

"So...do you think your mother loves you?"

Caleb thought for a minute and accepted that despite his accusations the day before he did believe she loved him. That's why the betrayal was all the more difficult to accept. He finally nodded.

"Do you believe she regrets the decision she made?"

He nodded again.

Doctor Collins leaned back. "Then the way I see it you have two choices. You can forgive her or not."

"It's not that simple," he said harshly.

The man studied Caleb without blinking. "Has Zach told you what happened to his leg?"

"You had to cut it off," Caleb said. "To keep him from drowning."

"Yes. It was the right decision, but it still haunts me. Sometimes in my dreams I'm not fast enough and he dies anyway in agony and fear. Sometimes he's not even drowning, I'm just doing it to him out of some evil compulsion. If I wanted to, right now, I could hear him begging me to stop and feel those cold waters push against me as I sawed through his leg. Every time I see the missing leg on the son I love and would die for it fills me with sadness and guilt. And then he laughs or smiles or plays, and I'm filled with such gratitude that he's still in my life. I suspect your mother feels the same."

Caleb thought about his mother as he had left her. Despondent and broken.

"Parenting is hard and no one tells you how to do it. If you're lucky you have good parents of your own to teach you, but even that's no guarantee of success. We're faced with terrible choices and some of them turn out well and some poorly. In every circumstance we can only do the best we can and pray it works out. Do you feel like your mother has done her best by you since then?"

"Yes," he said softly.

"I'm going to talk to you like I would my own son and hope you don't mind. This world is hard and we all get bloodied and beat down by something. Ugliness and nastiness and cruelty and tragedy are everywhere...but there is beauty through it all. You must cling to the beauty and goodness, or you'll just become angry and bitter."

Caleb saw a Monarch butterfly land on the hummingbird vine outside. Its delicate wings slowly opened and closed. He turned back to the man as Doctor Collins touched his hand.

"You matter despite what happened to you and despite the scars you carry. Just like my son. Something else you should know, your mother could have given you up for adoption even after everything…but she didn't. She kept you as a single mother and that's not an easy thing especially for a teenage girl. She did something terrible out of desperation and obviously regretted it. I don't know her, but I urge you to think about her as a person and all she has done for you. There aren't many people in this world who truly love us, so don't throw that away without careful consideration."

A car door slammed in the driveway and Caleb heard Zach and his sister laughing about something.

"One last thing," Doctor Collins stood. "We tend to think it is our actions that define us, but I have found far more often it is our reactions. So, like I asked earlier…what are you going to do about it?"

***

Caleb stayed for dinner at the Collins' house and then played in Zach's room until it got late. He made his way slowly down dark quiet streets that were beginning to feel chilly in the evenings. Letting himself into Mister McDaniel's house he found the old man sitting there reading. Mister McDaniel set the book down and pulled off reading glasses.

"Are you okay?" he asked.

"I'm fine," Caleb said climbing the stairs. "I'm tired, going to bed."

"Caleb?" the old man said from the bottom of the stairs.

He stopped at the door to the guest bedroom but didn't turn around. The last thing Caleb wanted to talk about was what had happened to him or even think about his mother.

"I wish you were my son," the old man said.

When Caleb turned to look down Mister McDaniel wasn't there.

Chapter 34

Thomas left the house early careful not to wake Caleb. He made sure to leave him a note along with a key to the house so the boy could lock up. Arriving at the courthouse, he waited in the lobby for Edwin Blake to be available. After about ten minutes his secretary waved him into the man's office.

"Who told you?" Edwin asked as soon as he walked into the room.

"Told me what? And good morning to you as well."

Edwin shook his head. "You know darn well what I'm talking about. Who told you that Frank Osborne was being released this morning? I presume that is why you're here."

"So, you *did* keep that info from me on purpose. I wondered why I didn't hear it from you."

"You know why!" Edwin leaning forward in his chair. "I can't have you doing something stupid that we'll both regret. You just need to stay away from that man. What's done is done."

Thomas perused the shelves of law books. "What's done is done, huh? What if I can't stay away from him? What if I can't live with him being out here free?"

Edwin threw his hands up in the air. "That's exactly the sort of thing I'm worried about and why I didn't tell you. Let's say you did confront Osbourne. What are you looking to get out if it? You're an old man and he's a hardened criminal. You'd be lucky if he didn't kill you…is that what you want? For him to kill you and go back to prison? For you to be some sort of martyr?"

"I'm not looking to be a martyr."

"Then stay away from that man," Edwin said pointing a large finger at him. "If he gives you any trouble, you let me know and I'll take care of it but don't try and take matters into your own hands. Understand?"

The secretary knocked quickly on the door before opening it. "Judge Harris wants to see you in his chambers. Says its urgent."

"Good grief," grunted Edwin climbing to his feet. "It's probably about that plea deal. I knew he wouldn't like it. Wants to be a hard ass on everything with elections coming up." He started out the door and turned back to Thomas. "We're not done. Just sit right there. I'll be right back."

Thomas sat for a few minutes looking at the books, the diplomas on the walls and the photos of Edwin with important people. He shifted in his seat to adjust the Colt .45 1911 pistol under his light jacket. He had asked to be issued one the very day after getting released from the Japanese prison camp and had carried it with him the rest of the war. Most chaplains refused to handle weapons, but by that point Thomas was determined to never be taken prisoner again. He would just keep shooting until they were forced to kill him.

He had imagined himself killing the prison guards many times, but he had never actually fired the pistol except for training. It was cleaned, oiled, and loaded and felt heavier than its weight. Thomas felt that anyone who saw him could tell it was on his hip, but no one gave any indication they knew of the pistol.

Standing, Thomas walked out of the prosecutor's office nodding to the secretary. Leaving his car parked on the courthouse curb he began to make his way across town towards the prison. He didn't hurry. Frank Osborne wasn't supposed to be released until shift change at ten thirty. He cheerfully greeted those he passed and absorbed all around him. It was a cloudy day but not too cold yet.

Thomas sat on the bus stop bench across from the prison entrance. He had been here many times before. In the early days after the trial and conviction he had sat on this very bench for hours trying to project his hate through those thick gray walls at Frank Osborne. Prayers and requests for divine vengeance had poured out of him and he had laid his heart bare. In some ways he had done his best work here on this bench, he thought.

A bus came and sat waiting for him to board. The driver honked at him annoyedly, but Thomas waved him on. The driver shook his head and drove away. Looking at his watch Thomas saw it was a quarter till eleven and he had a moment of panic.

What if they let him out early? What if he is already gone? Could Edwin have orchestrated that just to preclude the very act he was preparing to commit? That old lawyer really wanted to keep me in his office longer. He bowed his head and closed his eyes. *God, please don't make me go searching for him,* and as nearly an afterthought, *Forgive me for what I am about to do.*

There were noises at the prison gate. A small door opened and a thin man stepped outside tentatively, like an animal released into the wild for the first time. His clothes were out of fashion by several decades.

"Bus stop is across the street," said a guard from inside the gate. "Best of luck and try not to get into any trouble." Not waiting for a response, the door slammed shut and locks grated loudly.

Frank Osborne was much older than Thomas remembered him. While Thomas had aged twenty years, it looked like Frank had aged fifty. He fought down the faint twinge of pity that rose in him.

The felon looked both ways and crossed over to the bus stop. He glanced at Thomas and then ignored him.

"Just got out, huh," said Thomas.

Frank turned to look at him. "Yeah, feels good."

"How long were you in for?"

"Over twenty years," the man said as if he were only comprehending this information himself.

"That's a long time," Thomas answered. "What'd you do?"

Frank stared at him with a hard stare. "Mind your own business, old man." He then turned back to await the next bus.

Thomas climbed to his feet and drew the pistol from the holster on his belt. He faced Frank pointing it at the man. "Do you regret what you did?"

The felon turned angrily. "Listen here, you old…" his voice trailed off as his eyes saw the .45.

"Candice and Jenny Lowe," Thomas said reverently. "That was their names. You took far more than twenty years from them…from me."

Frank's eyes went back and forth between the pistol and Thomas. "You're that old priest aren't ya?" Then he smiled hesitantly. "Ain't no priest gonna kill nobody."

"I'm not a priest anymore." His finger tightened on the trigger.

The killer's eyes got larger and he held his hands out to his side. "What do you want? I served my time."

"I want…I want you to ask me to forgive you," the pistol was shaking and Thomas heard his own voice as if from outside himself. "So that I might forgive you. Take away the retribution you are due from me. Ask for my forgiveness with all your heart and I won't have to do this, but you have to ask for it first. That is how forgiveness works."

Frank stared at the pistol for a few long moments and then up at Thomas. A smile broke his face and he chuckled. "You're a crazy old man. Looks like a nice day, I think I'll stretch my legs." He then turned and began walking down the hill towards the center of town.

"Tell me you're sorry!" Thomas yelled at his back. "Ask me to forgive you!"

The man kept walking and held up both hands with the middle fingers sticking up.

"Lord forgive me," Thomas pointed the pistol at the killer's back and pulled on the trigger. His hands were shaking and he couldn't seem to get a grip on the pistol. He took it into both hands.

Are you my servant or his?

Screaming Thomas pointed the gun at the heavens and pulled the trigger over and over again until it stopped firing. Then he dropped the empty .45 to the ground and covered his face. Tears burned tracks in his cheeks. The world was strangely quiet after the thunder of gunfire.

He finally lifted his head and saw Frank Osborne sprawled on the ground. For a moment Thomas wondered if he had actually shot the man. Then he saw him clutching at his chest. The old man walked over slowly and looked down at the felon.

Out of habit he reached for his pocket Bible, rosary, and oil for last rites, but only the rosary was in his pocket. And he was no longer a priest.

"My heart," Frank moaned. "Call an ambulance, don't think I'm going to make it."

Thomas knelt down beside him the rosary in his hands. "Are you Catholic?"

"My *heart*," Frank whispered looking at Thomas like he was crazy.

"What is your faith?" Thomas asked and realized he was completely calm. "I can also pray with you if you are Protestant or Jewish. In the army we had to multitask as chaplains, but I need to know your faith."

"Faith?" the man croaked. "I don't even believe in God."

"Well, you're getting ready to. Best be prepared."

"I don't want to die," there was now real fear in Frank's eyes. "I'm not ready."

Thomas almost stood and walked away. He pictured Candice and Jenny and wanted to take joy in this moment but found he couldn't. All he could feel was profound sadness.

Frank grabbed his hand. "Help me, please."

"No," the old man answered and tried to pull his hand away, but the dying man's grip was still strong and desperate.

Help him, said a voice in his head.

Thomas knew what was being asked of him and he rebelled against it with every fiber of his being.

Are you my servant or his?

Thomas looked up at the gray clouds and then back down at the man before him. "I am yours, Lord. Always yours." He gripped the other man's hand and put his palm on Frank Osborne's chest. "Do you accept that you are a sinner in rebellion against Almighty God and are deserving of death?"

Frank nodded.

"Do you believe that all have sinned and fallen short of the glory of God and that he wants none of us to be lost and has prepared a way for you to be saved?"

Another nod.

"Do you believe that Jesus Christ is the Son of God and died for our sins? That he who was blameless took all our punishment upon himself so that it would not fall upon us?"

"Yes," the man whispered.

Thomas took a deep breath and looked into Frank's fading eyes. "Do you accept the free gift of Christ's salvation and renounce evil? Do you accept Christ as your Lord and Savior and invite Him into your life and your heart?"

"Yes," smiled Frank up at him. Tears were streaming out of his eyes and there was an aura of peace about him.

Thomas made the sign of the cross over the man. "May God's love, mercy, and peace be upon you. May He hold you in His hand and walk with you all the days of your life. May He welcome you into His eternal presence. Amen."

The sun broke out from behind the clouds as Frank's hand went limp and his head dropped lifeless to the side. Thomas sat back on his heels wiping the tears from his face. He was about to climb to his feet when he heard yelling and running feet from the front gate of the prison.

A moment later he was tackled and crushed to the ground under uniformed bodies.

Chapter 35

Caleb woke again in a bed that wasn't his, but the confusion didn't last as long as before. He knew he was in Mister McDaniel's guest bedroom. He looked outside the window and saw that it was going to be a gray overcast day. Also, judging by the morning light, he was going to be late for school again.

Unhurriedly, he went downstairs expecting to find the old man. The stillness told him he was alone in the house. Looking out the back door window Caleb saw the garage door was up and the car that usually sat there was gone. Then he spotted the envelope on the table with his name on the outside. A house key sat next to it.

He opened the letter and pulled out the piece of paper. The old man's handwriting was even, neat, and flowed with a subtle grace that Caleb's artistic eye could appreciate. Standing in the kitchen light he read the words.

Caleb,

I might be away for a while and I don't know for how long. You, and your family if needed, are welcome in my house as long as you want. I consider you family now, the only family I have left.

I want you to know that you are not a mistake. What has happened to you changes nothing. Our scars do not define us. Stop trying to be anything other than what God made you to be. Stop hiding who you really are. Let the world feel the weight of you and let the world deal with it.

Never forget that God loves you and delights in you…as do I.

Your friend, Thomas McDaniel.

P.S. Don't judge your mother too harshly. You haven't lived long enough to face terrible choices but you likely will.

Caleb sat down at the table and read the letter again. Then he stared out the window. Where could the old man be going? He put the letter carefully away and placed it in his back pocket. Using the house key he locked the front door. At the end of the driveway, he expected to turn right towards school. Instead, his feet took him to the left.

Approaching his house, he saw their car half in the driveway and half off in the yard. The back end kept bumping into the base of a nearby tree lightly and then going forward again until the front of the car hit the corner of the garage. It kept going back and forth and the woman behind the wheel had a frantic look in her eyes.

"Grandma!" Caleb called running up to her window. "What are you doing?"

She didn't look at him, keeping her eyes in the rearview mirror as if lining up for another go at getting the car out. "Got to go pick up Bev at kindergarten. I don't want her to think I forgot about her."

Caleb watched until he saw she had her foot on the brake before he reached in quickly and put the gear shift in park. He then turned the ignition off and pulled the keys out.

She looked at him for the first time. "What do you think you're doing, young man?"

"Just come on inside, Grandma," he opened the car door, and she looked at him suspiciously.

"Caleb? Why aren't you in school?"

He took her by the arm noticing her mismatched clothing and slippers. "Come on inside." She stepped out of the car and let him lead her up the porch stairs. Inside he was stunned at how messy everything had gotten in only a few days. Guiding his grandmother to her bedroom he eased her onto her bed.

"Just going to rest my eyes," she said pulling her legs up under her. The confusion and stress eased out of her face. Caleb picked up a blanket from the foot of the bed and spread it over her.

Standing there looking at her he thought of the car and wondered if he could get it back into the garage. He then realized if the car was there then his mother was at home. That she hadn't gone to work.

Listening he heard nothing. Walking softly down the hallway he saw her bedroom door cracked open with nothing but darkness within. Caleb saw the door couldn't close fully because the door frame was splinted. He pushed the door open and stepped inside.

It took a few moments for his eyes to adjust. Finally, he saw a woman curled up on the bed her knees up close to her chin. Caleb thought at first she was sleeping but saw eyes looking at him. She then buried her face in the pillow and started moaning.

Crossing the room quickly he sat on the bed and gathered her into his arms. She fought him and tried to draw away.

"It's okay, mom," he said softly. "It's okay."

She stopped struggling and covered her face. "I'm sorry. So sorry."

He stroked her hair. "I know, it's okay. I'm sorry too. You did the best you could."

"I didn't know it was you," she sobbed.

"I know," he said holding her. "It's all going to be okay."

Caleb held his mother for a long time as she cried against him.

Chapter 36

Most of the time Edwin Blake loved the law. It was simple and clean. It kept civilized society from descending into violence and chaos. People like him were the ones who made it possible for kids to play on the streets at night and for families to leave their doors unlocked.

Today was different, conflicted somehow. He didn't feel good about what he was going to have to do, what he had already had to do over the last few weeks. Thomas McDaniel looked over at him from beside Chad Varn, his public defender and smiled serenely.

Damn fool has no idea what he's in for, Edwin thought.

Judge Harris finally stopped shuffling through papers and looked up at the courtroom. "Having reviewed the available evidence and heard pre-trial arguments I determine this case can proceed to trial." He looked down at Thomas. "On the charges of manslaughter of Frank Osborne how do you plead?"

There was whispered discussion among Thomas and Chad. Edwin could tell there was some sort of disagreement.

"How does the defense plead?" Judge Harris asked again the annoyance starting to bleed into his voice.

"Just a moment please, your honor," said Chad.

Judge Harris sighed and looked at Edwin with exasperation. "Mister Varn," he said after a few minutes, "it is a relatively simple –"

"Guilty," said Thomas McDaniel. "I plead guilty, your honor."

"No, he doesn't," Chad said quickly.

"Oh, yes, I do, young man," Thomas answered.

"Defense approach the bench," Judge Harris said and both Chad and Edwin walked up in front of him. "Is your client mentally incapacitated?"

"No, your honor," Chad said resolutely.

The judge held one hand out towards Thomas. "Then you have no grounds to deny his chosen plea. Does he fully understand the ramifications of a guilty plea?"

"He does, your honor," Thomas said loudly and they all looked at the man sitting contentedly.

"There it is then," said Judge Harris shooing them away and back to their tables. He then looked out over the courtroom. "Given the guilty plea of the defense we will forego a trial and proceed directly to sentencing."

Chad rose to his feet. "Your honor, given my client's age, his status as a decorated World War Two veteran and former Roman Catholic priest, as well as the emotional circumstances of this case, I would like to ask the court to forego prison time and assign probation and house arrest."

Edwin rose. "The prosecution concurs, your honor."

Judge Harris looked at Edwin in surprise and shook his head. Edwin felt a sinking feeling in his stomach and remembered that this was an election year for the judge. Judge Harris had made his career and name by being tough on criminals.

"I have taken your requests into consideration," the judge said, "but this is a case of blatant violence in our town. Mister McDaniel went to the local prison with a pistol intending to murder Frank Osborne upon his release. Mister Osborne had served his time and by law was owed an opportunity to reintegrate himself into society. Thomas McDaniel took that from him, and he is fortunate that we are not considering charges of attempted murder."

He gave Edwin a sharp look at this point. There had been several heated arguments behind closed doors between the two of them on this very topic. Thomas had not shot Frank Orborne, but it was likely the gunshots had brought on the heart attack that ultimately killed him.

"We cannot have vigilante justice in our town," Judge Harris was speaking directly to Thomas at this point. "I'm dismayed that a man of your background would even consider such a thing." He motioned to Chad and Thomas with an upward waving of his hand.

Both rose to their feet.

"Thomas McDaniel I sentence you to twenty-five years in a state penitentiary." He banged his gavel and looked over at the bailiff. "Remand the defendant into custody. Court is in recess."

"All rise," said a loud voice near the judge and everyone stood to their feet as the judge left the room.

Edwin watched as hand cuffs were placed on Thomas' wrists. He expected the man to look afraid but instead he had a slight smile on his face. As they led the old man away, Thomas locked eyes with Edwin and gave him a nod.

"It's a damn shame," Chad said walking over to him.

"Guilty plea!" Edwin turned on him furious. "What the hell were you thinking? A jury would *never* have convicted him if it had gone to trial!"

"I know," said Chad. "I told him that very thing, but he insisted. Said God was in control and had a plan for his life. There was no reasoning with him. It was almost as if he wanted to go to prison."

Edwin shook his head gazing in the direction they had taken Thomas. An unfamiliar feeling of powerlessness weighed him down. "Old fool."

Chad handed Edwin a sealed envelope. "He prepared these ahead of time and asked me to pass them along to you. Wanted to also tell you he was sorry for letting you down and grateful for your friendship over the years. I have to say it is a first for me that a convicted defendant thanks the prosecutor."

"He was one of a kind," Edwin said taking the envelope. Chad nodded to him and walked out of the courtroom.

Opening the envelope he found two pieces of paper. The first asked him to take whatever legal steps were required to ensure Caleb Woods and his family could stay at his house and use his property while he was in prison. Thomas also specified that he renounced ownership of the .45 pistol he had recently used and for the police to dispose of it however they chose.

"Who the hell is Caleb Woods?" Edwin said as he opened the other letter. It was Thomas' last will and testament. He had left the house and his possessions to the same Caleb Woods. The contents of his savings account at First Federal Bank and of his checking account at Farmers Bank were to go to Saint Matthew's Church.

Edwin sighed deeply, put the pieces of paper back in the envelope, and walked out of the courtroom.

Chapter 37

Caleb thought it felt strange for his mother to be with him in Miss Simms' classroom. At least it was a Saturday morning and none of the other kids were around. His mom had finally agreed to meet with Caleb's teacher, especially after he shared his drawings with her and showed her what he was reading. By this point it was difficult to leave his grandmother at home by herself for very long, but a neighbor had agreed to sit with her while they attended the teacher meeting.

The last few weeks had been filled with a newness that was difficult to describe. For the first time in his life, Caleb felt like his mother really saw him. She talked to him and asked his opinion on things. Wanted to know what he liked and didn't and why. What he was interested in. As if she were trying to get to know him. Almost without realizing it they had become closer, not necessarily despite what had happened but because of it. It was as if all their lives some invisible presence had kept them separated and it was suddenly gone. Perhaps most amazingly of all, they started going to church together.

Thomas McDaniel's conviction was the talk of the town for a few days. Caleb wanted to go visit him but couldn't as a minor. Besides, inmates were not allowed visitors the first ninety days of incarceration. The brief interaction the night he had come back from the Collins' house was the last time he had actually seen the old priest or spoken to him. He wished he had more time with him. Thinking of the old man made him think of the letter Mister McDaniel had written him. The letter made him think of his deformity. A deformity that Caleb now thought of as part of himself. He had decided against the surgery for now, but Doctor Collins told him it was always an option if he changed his mind.

Let the world feel the weight of you and let the world deal with it.

Caleb's mother fidgeted nervously as his teacher sat down with them.

"Good morning, it is so nice to meet you," his teacher said. "Thank you for coming in on a Saturday."

"I was off this morning," his mother said, "it was not a problem."

"First things first, I suppose. Your son is highly intelligent as are most dyslexics" Denise Simms told Beverly. "But he is behind in nearly all subjects and this school system's ability to deal with anything outside of the norm is very limited."

"What is a dyslexic?" his mother asked.

Miss Simms explained it to her. How it was a newly discovered way of thinking and learning that made certain basic tasks like reading initially very challenging. Most dyslexics were dismissed as unintelligent, mentally disabled, or simply poor readers early in childhood and never recovered.

"Can he recover?" Beverly darted her eyes anxiously at her son.

"I believe so. He's already made incredible progress," the teacher replied, "but it will be difficult here. Caleb doesn't belong in a special education class, but it is the sole option available in this school district. Most school districts if I'm being completely honest. Our only chance for him to *try* and catch up is me working with him after school for a few hours each day. Meanwhile his fellow classmates are learning and advancing in new areas eight hours a day."

"So, he might have a chance to graduate high school?" his mother asked tentatively.

Miss Simms laughed before catching herself. "I'm sorry, ma'am. Caleb is intelligent enough and talented enough to attend and graduate college if he wants. But we have a number of hurdles to overcome."

"College?" she said softly and reached out to take Caleb's hand. As far as she knew no one in her family had ever even gone to college.

"Yes, but I'm afraid that will be very difficult here in his current situation."

"What's to be done?" his mother asked.

Miss Simms took a deep breath before continuing. "There is a small private prep school in Lexington. I sent them some of Caleb's artwork and test results and they are extremely interested. They have had success dealing with students who are challenged in certain ways and have recently hired a counselor who specializes in dyslexia."

"We would have to move?" his mother asked confused.

"Not exactly. This is boarding school, Miss Woods. Caleb would live there during the school year. Full-time. With the other students."

His mother looked back and forth between Miss Simms and Caleb. "Going away? On his own? He's just a…he's so…"

"I can do it, Mom," Caleb said squeezing her hand. "I want to do it."

She studied him closely. "You already knew about this?"

"I told him," Miss Simms said. "I apologize for not talking to you first, but I didn't want to get anyone's hopes up if he wasn't interested." She placed a trifold color brochure on the table before them. The title said Johnson Academy. Underneath this was a motto, *Where Young Men Reach Their Full Potential.*

His mother picked it up and thumbed through the pages of pictures of brownstone buildings, manicured lawns, and smiling students. "It looks expensive."

"You don't have to worry about that," Denise said. "I was able to secure a special scholarship for Caleb through my alma mater. It will cover tuition, lodging, and meals. It's an excellent school and a very good opportunity for Caleb."

"But, he'll have to go away," his mother said softly while looking at the brochure in his hands.

"For a while," Caleb said. "I'll be home for holidays and summer breaks."

"When would he leave?" his mother asked.

"As soon as possible," Miss Simms answered. "The semester has already started and he's going to have some catching up to do anyway. There won't be a break for Thanksgiving, but you'll have him home for Christmas."

His mother turned to him and her eyes shifted up towards his head. "Boys can be mean and you'll be all alone up there."

"I can handle it, Mom. Don't worry."

"Is this something you want? Truly? Have you thought about it?"

Caleb nodded and smiled. "They have a great art program. I'll even learn how to *paint*."

His mother pulled out a tissue and wiped her eyes. She sighed heavily and looked at Miss Simms. "Is this the best thing for him? I want to do right by my son, but I don't know what that is. I'm always so worried for him."

"That's understandable, Miss Woods. It's obvious that you love Caleb and have done an incredible job raising him. He's a fine young man and has the potential to be much more." Miss Simms pointed at the brochure. "I firmly believe, *this* is the right thing for your son. Change and growth are always hard. But this, *this* is his best opportunity."

His mother stared at the brochure. Her hands were shaking slightly. Finally, she nodded and wiped her eyes some more. "Okay."

"Okay?" asked Denise looking back and forth between Caleb and his mother.

"Okay," said his mother meeting Miss Simms' eyes. Fear and hope were heavy on her face.

"Okay," said Caleb. He stood and wrapped his mother in a tight hug. "Thank you," he whispered in her ear. "For everything."

Chapter 38

Beverly was proud of herself. She had hardly cried at all while dropping off Caleb. Now that she was driving back to Cairn she couldn't seem to stop. Not tears of shame but clean tears. Tears that felt as if they were cleaning her soul. Washing away the last remnants of festering secrets and hidden regrets. She was sad Caleb was at school, but she knew it was a fresh beginning, for both of them.

The drive back to Cairn was scenic and pleasant. Beverly couldn't remember the last time she had gone on a long drive anywhere. It also felt a little scary being on her own, but also freeing somehow.

It had been a week since they were forced to put her mother into a nursing home. Helen had wandered out into the street in front of a car and almost got hit. Her doctor determined her dementia was rapidly getting worse. To pay the exorbitant cost of the nursing home, Beverly had been forced to sign over ownership of her mother's home. Now they were residing in Thomas McDaniel's much nicer home. Beverly didn't know how long they would be there, but given the old man's conviction it would likely be for many years.

Caleb. It all came back to Caleb. How could she have missed so much for so long? What would have happened if people hadn't come into their lives at just the right moment? Beverly used to imagine what her life could have been like if she hadn't gotten pregnant. Now she imagined what Caleb's life could be like in the future. Maybe hers too. She was still young. Perhaps she would make friends. Join that ladies church group. Get her GED. If her son could be brave and do hard things then how could she not at least try herself?

Driving through the hills the autumn leaves were beginning to fall. This had always been her favorite time of the year. The brilliant reds, yellows, and oranges made the world so cheerful even if it signified the coming of winter. She had planned to simply go home…Mister McDaniel's home that is, but thinking of doing hard things turned her towards Green Villages on the north edge of Cairn.

Beverly had not been to the nursing home since they moved her mother there. Helen Woods was difficult to get along with even before dementia. Now every interaction was a roll of the dice. Would she know who she was or think she was a teenager again? Would she be catatonic or bitterly cruel? Would she even recognize her own daughter?

She parked and walked slowly to the front desk to sign in. Beverly made her way down the halls smelling of antiseptic and air freshener. The sound of a television game show could be heard from a distant part of the facility. Stopping at her mother's room she gathered her courage before walking inside.

The room was small but better than a larger room with double occupancy. Beverly knew her mother would be happier with some privacy. She had always been that way, and the sale of the house had covered the extra cost. As many of her mother's familiar belongings as possible had been moved here. The beautiful quilt her mother sewed years before covered a neatly made bed. Someone had obviously done that for her.

There was no sign of Helen Woods and Beverly stepped back out into the hallway. A passing woman in the facility's pale blue uniform saw the look on her face.

"She's sitting out on the back veranda," the woman told her without breaking stride. She pointed down the hall. "Helen likes to sit outside when the weather is nice."

Beverly wondered if the woman was getting Helen confused with someone else. She had never known her mother to sit outside voluntarily. Making her way down the hallway, Beverly pushed open the outside door and indeed found her mother sitting in a wheelchair looking out over a nearby field framed in rolling hills. An old man brooded on the other side of the veranda but paid Beverly no notice.

She pulled up a nearby chair and sat down. "Hello, Mom. It's Beverly."

Her mother didn't look at her. "Paw went rabbit hunting. If he gets some we'll have stew for dinner. He'll skin 'em but I'll have to do the cleaning."

"How are you doing, they treating you okay?"

A disturbed look came over her mother's face. "Mabel's stopped laying eggs. If she doesn't start laying 'em again maw will put her in the cook pot. Mabel's my favorite."

Beverly sighed and looked out over the hills. "I took Caleb off to school today. He's in Lexington now." She fought the urge to cry. It seemed like tears were always a possibility in any situation these days. "It looks like a really nice place."

Her mother smiled. "I'm going to wear my yellow sundress to the dance on Saturday. I hope Berry Pickens asks me to dance with him."

"You were right, Mom. About Caleb. You were right all along. I shouldn't have babied him. I should have opened my eyes and *seen* him, but I was always so busy. So worried about *my* life, *my* problems."

Helen turned to look at her. "You got a cigarette?"

"No, Mother. Cigarettes aren't allowed here. Although I honestly couldn't tell you why. I don't think you have to worry about lung cancer at this point."

Her mother said nothing, just stared off at the hills.

"I know we didn't always get along and that I wasn't always a good daughter, but I remember you looking out for me when you could. I remember you walking and holding my hand when I was little. I would sit in your lap until I fell asleep." The tears were falling now and she let them. "I just wanted to say…I'm sorry about everything, and I'm sorry you ended up this way."

Her mother leaned forward and squinted into the distance. "If we don't get the corn in soon it's going to rot."

"I gotta go, Mom," Beverly touched the woman's arm. "I'll try to come visit again soon."

At Beverly's touch her mother turned to stare at her. Her eyes showed confusion, and then she smiled and reached out a hand to touch Beverly gently on her cheek. "I'm sorry. I don't know who you are, but I know you're someone I love." She then dropped her hand and turned back to the view.

Beverly rose slowly and made her way down the hall and out into the parking lot. She fumbled with her keys and barely made it into the car before a lifetime of emotion poured out of her.

Chapter 39

Thomas had determined after Camp O'Donnell was liberated that he would never allow himself to be a prisoner again. To never be at the complete mercy of another human being. To never suffer such degradation, fear, and loathing. He knew firsthand what humans would do to other humans when humanity was removed from the equation.

Yet here he was. This time by choice. Thomas supposed he should be afraid. Instead, a sense of profound peace had filled him since Frank Osborne's salvation. He could feel the very Spirit of God coursing through his veins and the joy was nearly boundless.

"What you smiling at, old man?"

Thomas turned to find an inmate with a wicked scar running down the side of his face. Several other rough men stood behind him watching. “Nothing in particular,” he answered.

Another inmate walked up from his left. “You’re that old priest that killed Frankie, aren’t you? The very day he was released. That’s cold.”

Thomas closed his eyes and lifted his hands up towards heaven. “Lord God Almighty, let your blessing and mercy be upon us all. Protect us from evil and help us to walk in your ways. Amen.”

When he opened his eyes he found all the men a full ten feet further away from him than when he had started the prayer. Most of them had a look of stunned fear in their eyes. “Jesus said, ‘Do not be afraid for I am with you even until the end of the age.’ He came to set us free and redeem the captives.”

“Shut up, old man,” came a cry from behind him but more people were gathering near Thomas.

He pointed at a man at random. “If a man is thrown into solitary for a week, is he any more a prisoner than the rest of us?”

“No,” came a few voices. Someone said, “We’re all still prisoners.”

"Exactly, my friends," Thomas nodded. "We are prisoners in here but so is the rest of the world, we are simply in a smaller prison."

"What the hell are you talking about?"

Thomas turned to regard them. "Hell is exactly what I'm talking about. And heaven. This world and this life is only the beginning. Eternity is our birthright. Jesus came and died so we could be free, be with him. Separation from God is a prison that leads to eternal damnation, but we can all be free. We can all live in the way we were originally meant to."

"What you talking about free?" came an angry voice. "I'm on a life sentence. Ain't ever getting out of here."

"Oh, but you will," Thomas said in the direction of the voice. "You will get out of here and you will spend eternity…somewhere. And this life is a millisecond compared to the billions upon billions of years and more you will spend in that place."

The man with the scar on his face pointed an angry finger at the priest. "We all know where we're going, no need for you to remind us."

"But you don't have to go there," Thomas smiled. "For all have sinned and fallen short of the glory of God.

He loves *you*," he pointed at the man, "and *you*," pointing at another, "and *you*. And all of us. So much so that he gave his only son as a sacrifice to atone for our sins that he might live with us forever."

"Don't no Jesus want anything to do with men like us!" came a cry.

"That's where you're wrong. The God of the universe loves you more deeply and completely than you can ever know. He yearns for you to turn to him. Forgiveness and salvation are at hand and God loves you." Thomas surveyed the confused faces. "God isn't mad at you. He might be disappointed. You may have made him sad, but he isn't mad at you. God is crazy about you. All of you."

Now there was nearly complete silence, and Thomas could even see some of the guards listening to him.

"Today," he cried, "is the day of salvation. I urge you brothers to not let this moment pass. The devil will tell you that you aren't worthy, that you're not good enough and don't deserve salvation and he's right. But good people don't get into heaven, forgiven people do."

"How can we be forgiven?" said a massive man with tattoos covering both arms.

"You ask for it," Thomas said simply. "We have all sinned against our Heavenly Father and he is waiting for us to return to him. Ask for his forgiveness and accept Jesus' free gift of salvation. He made that sacrifice for each of you."

"Move away!" came a guard's voice over a bullhorn. "No gathering!"

The men slowly began to break off into smaller groups and go back to their previous activities, but many kept looking back at Thomas. He felt confident that he would be talking with many of them soon.

"Where do you think you are?" asked a one-eyed man standing nearby. "This is a prison, not some church service. You best figure it out."

Thomas nodded at him. "I know exactly where I am. This is not my first time in prison, and that one was far worse than this one. I promise you that."

A smaller man came over and took him by the elbow and led him away. "You keep that stuff up, and you're going to get killed."

Thomas turned to the man. "We all die sometime and will be raised to life or death. I can think of no better way to die than trying to save God's lost sheep. I can hope of no better way to leave this life than with Jesus' name on my lips."

"Who are you to talk to us about God, killer?"

He looked at the surrounding men. The lost sheep, the forgotten, the forsaken, the hopeless, the shamed. "I am a priest of the Most High God and I am right where I am supposed to be, for He has sent me to proclaim to you the Good News."

Thomas felt a warmth spread through him and could sense God smiling on him. He began to laugh with joy.

For you created my innermost being; you knit me together in my mother's womb. I praise you because I am fearfully and wonderfully made; your works are wonderful, I know that full well. My frame was not hidden from you when I was made in the secret place. When I was woven together in the depths of the earth, your eyes saw my unformed body. All the days ordained for me were written in your book before one of them came to be.
Psalms 139:13-16

For everyone who calls on the name of the Lord will be saved.
Romans 10:13

Afterword

This book is a work of fiction but God's love for you is more real than anything in this universe. He sees you and is for you. The Creator of Heaven and Earth seeks most desperately to care for you as a loving and happy father… if you will let Him.

The Good News that Jesus and the early church preached was of the coming Kingdom of God. This is a place meant for all of God's children. A place free of sin, doubt, sickness, death, pain, remorse, shame, loneliness, and guilt. A place of perfect harmony and love with God, His creation, and all those who acknowledge Him. A cosmically vast place where we will worship, love, fellowship, explore, play, learn, party, sing, dance, laugh, create, eat, drink, build, work, and rest. All to the glory of God and all of it making Him smile.

Goodness is coming. Something better is coming. Eternity awaits.

But do not be fooled into believing the lie that all will enter into God's presence when they die. Jesus taught very clearly that only those who accept His free gift of salvation, repent of their sins, and call Him their Lord will enter into His presence. He would not force people who reject Him to spend eternity with Him. For those people eternity will be a place completely devoid of God and of His love, goodness, and light. Rest assured that after we die we will all spend eternity somewhere.

I urge you with all my heart to seek out God. To acknowledge Him as Lord of your life and let Him welcome you into His loving arms. We have all fallen short and are deserving of death, but Jesus made a way through His death, burial, and resurrection for us to be saved.

If you do not know Jesus Christ as your Lord and Savior, I implore you to invite Him into your life. To ask Him to forgive you for your sins and accept Christ's sacrifice on your behalf. To study His Holy Word starting with the Gospel of John.

God wants to welcome you home with loving arms. Do not put off this decision even one more minute.

Today is the day of salvation. Eternity awaits.

Acknowledgements

This book, more than others I have written, was a labor of love. The story of Caleb, Thomas, Helen, Beverly, and Denise could not have been possible without first God's inspiration and love.

Second, a number of people provided beta reading, editing, and content recommendations that made this book much better than if it had only come from my mind and hands. Special thanks to my wife Kristin, my mother Betty Hill, my sister Shanna Dowdy, my in-laws Sherman and Diane Chaudoin, my niece Jaime Chaudoin, my brother-in-Christ Brad Copeland, our dear friend Tina Via, and ultra avid reader extraordinaire Faith Johnson.

And last but not least I want to thank you reader for picking this book up and giving it a chance. I sincerely hope you enjoyed it and that it was worth your time.

Until next time…